Hard Rain Falling

by

Wendell Logan

PublishAmerica
Baltimore

© 2007 by Wendell Logan.
All rights reserved. No part of this book may be reproduced, stored in a retrieval system or transmitted in any form or by any means without the prior written permission of the publishers, except by a reviewer who may quote brief passages in a review to be printed in a newspaper, magazine or journal.

First printing

All characters appearing in this work are fictitious. Any resemblance to real persons, living or dead, is purely coincidental.

ISBN: 1-4241-8149-6
PUBLISHED BY PUBLISHAMERICA, LLLP
www.publishamerica.com
Baltimore

Printed in the United States of America

To Vincie: Who always believed

I would like to thank my many friends and family who encouraged me to write this story. They know who they are.

Martha:
Mark:

Hope you enjoy the book as much as we enjoy your hospitality when we are in Santa Fe.

Wendell

Chapter I

"You should be ok, if it doesn't rain on you," Pat's father said as he stopped the car and let us out on the black pavement.

It was June 1, 1963, and I had just finished my sophomore year of college in Oklahoma. We were about eighteen hundred miles from our destination, which was Strasborg, Washington. Since Pat and I both were almost broke we decided to hitchhike all the way. Strasborg is only about twenty-five miles from Walla Walla and we both had summer jobs there, working in a pea-canning factory. I'm sure you have seen the product on your supermarket shelf and eaten them far more often than you care to remember, if you ever ate lunch in a public school cafeteria.

We got our baggage out of the back, shook hands with Pat's father and began walking the hundred yards or so that joined the access road to the main highway. A hard and surprisingly cold rain began to fall before we had covered the distance. Whenever it rained like that in Oklahoma I would always think of a friend of mine who would comment that it was raining like a cow pissing on a flat rock. It seemed like an appropriate comment at the moment.

We must have looked pitiful, standing there soaked through, for in a couple of minutes a big green Cadillac came screeching by us. The driver slammed on his brakes just as he got to us, but it still took him well over a hundred feet or so to stop with the big car fishtailing the last fifty feet. Pat and I looked at each other for a moment, not sure if we wanted to ride with someone driving so carelessly. But, the rain was really coming down so we picked up our bags and began to run, afraid the driver might change his mind and leave us stranded.

"Where you headed?" he asked through teeth that were clamped tight around a King Edward cigar.

"Washington State," Pat and I both answered at the same time.

"Well, can't take you very far, only going as far as Wichita myself."

"That's fine," Pat said. "We just wanted out of the rain."

The driver was Carl from Wichita, and he was a real talker. He talked about the weather and how the rain slowed him down. He kept the speedometer on eighty-five and it was raining so hard I could barely see the white divider on the highway. I wondered what this guy did on dry pavement. When he got through talking about the weather, he talked about the Cadillac. He made it sound as if he was talking about a woman. I always wonder why men refer to their cars and guns as "she" or "her." I was glad I had taken the back seat so I wouldn't be forced to listen to this guy and his love affair with the car.

When it came to talking, Pat did a pretty good job himself, but this guy was in a class all alone. About all Pat could manage was a "yeah" or "is that right?" Since I had known Pat I had never seen him at a loss for words, and I could see the frustration building. I loved to see Pat getting a dose of his own medicine, as Carl kept rambling, never giving him a chance to get into the conversation.

After Carl finished telling us about how great the Cadillac was, he started on his job. From what I could tell, he was some sort of electronics salesman for a supply firm in Wichita. He was returning from a week-long sales trip to Oklahoma City and Tulsa and was in a hurry to get home. I was more interested in trying to get dry and listening to the radio, where a country western singer was singing about his cheating wife. I settled comfortably into the soft leather seats that smelled faintly of aftershave lotion and smoke from cheap cigars.

After about thirty minutes, the rain had almost stopped and the driver put the top back on the Cadillac. We were going so fast, the light rain whipped over the windshield of the big car and over our heads. It was like being protected by an invisible umbrella.

It took less than an hour to cover the distance to Wichita. Carl let us out at a gas station on an access road, since it looked like a good place to catch a ride. Pat and I flipped a coin to see who would go ahead. We thought it would be easier to catch a ride if we separated. We had decided to pick out our destination each day and agreed to reunite at night, unless one of us got lucky and caught a ride that covered a longer distance. As it turned out, we did get separated, but it wasn't because one of us had caught a long ride.

Pat lost the flip, so he picked up his bag and started walking. As soon as he got to the interstate, an old black Chevrolet pulled over and I saw him jump in. Pat was always lucky like that. I felt sorry for the guy who stopped since I knew Pat was ready to talk someone's ear off after having listened to the guy in the Cadillac for the last hour.

I must have asked a dozen drivers at the gas station for a ride in the next hour, all without any luck. Finally, I decided to walk up to the interstate and try my luck there. I had been standing there about ten minutes, when a kid in a blue Chevy Bel Air pulled over and motioned for me to get in.

He was seventeen and his name was Wade. He was skinny, with red pimples and horn-rimmed glasses that kept sliding down on his hawk nose. He had a funny way of tilting his head back and wrinkling his nose up to get them back in place. I disliked him immediately.

We hadn't gone far before I knew I'd made a mistake. The kid was fruity, a real honest queer. He started in innocently enough, asking where I was going, the usual small talk. He was real impressed when he found out I planned to thumb all the way to Washington. Guess it didn't take much to impress folks in Wichita.

"That's one hell of a long way," he breathed, a little too heavily I thought. "Why you want to hitchhike?"

"It's cheap," I said, "like me."

"Trying to save money, huh?" he deducted. "I know what you mean. I ain't got a pot to piss in." The way he said it, I knew I was supposed to be impressed, but there wasn't anything impressive about this kid.

"That's right," I muttered, trying to be nice.

"Yeah," he continued, encouraged by my response. "Even the car ain't mine. The old man would croak now if he knew I had it out. I got to get to Hutchinson though."

He waited for me to ask him what was so important in Hutchinson. I didn't ask so he told me.

"I've got this hot little chick, just can't get enough of it," he went on, not at all deterred by my lack of interest. "She called me this morning and asked me to come on up."

"That right?" I replied, knowing he was going to tell me all about his sex life anyway.

"What about yourself?" he asked suddenly.

"What about me?" I said, although knowing full well what he was getting at.

"Bet you get a lot, huh? Being in college and all. I hear college is the place to be, all right."

"Yeah," I said, "it's the place to be if you want an education."

He laughed loudly; the way people do when they are nervous and unsure of themselves. All the while he was punching the buttons on the radio going from one station to another. His preference seemed to be country western and as soon as one song ended he would punch a button hoping to catch another song. He was making me nervous and I thought about telling him to stop and let me out, but I really wanted to ride as far as I could.

"You married?" he wanted to know.

"No, I'm not married," I answered, wondering if it was really any of his business.

"Well, if you ain't married and you don't take out the chicks at school, what do you do for it?" He was an inquisitive kid and he was getting on my nerves.

"I manage," I shrugged. I didn't like myself for answering. It only seemed to encourage him.

"Yeah, I bet you do," he said with a wink at me. "You like the boys maybe, is that it, cause if you do I can go that route myself."

I turned to face him in the car seat. "Look, kid," I said, "you don't need to tell me you're queer, it's written all over you. I knew when you picked me up you were a fruit and now I'm going to tell you something. Maybe you don't know this, but it's legal as hell for me to beat the crap out of you and tell everyone you made a pass at me. So, if you don't know that, you better learn it fast before someone does just that."

He shut up.

I knew that what I had told him was pure bullshit, but it was all I could think of to shut him up. Besides that, I was tired of all of his questions and heavy breathing.

We rode in silence for about fifteen minutes until he said, "The turnoff to Hutchinson is just up the road."

"Great," I replied. "You can let me out anytime."

The turnoff was at a crossroads and there was a gas station, combination garage and what looked like a run-down beer joint on opposite corners. An old black Chevrolet was parked in front of the bar and when I got closer, I recognized it as the one that had picked Pat up in Wichita. I crossed the street and headed in the direction of the tavern. Pat was sitting at one end of the bar with a bottle of Coors in front of him. An old man with enormous shoulders and thick gray hair that curled out from underneath a greasy rain hat sat next to him. I figured he must be the driver of the Chevy. He looked as old and beat up as the car he was driving.

"Hey," Pat yelled when he spotted me, "come here. Want you to meet a friend of mine." Pat was like that. No matter how long he had known someone, they were always his friends. It mattered little to him that people did not always feel the same way about him.

During the year that we were roommates I had to save his ass more than once because he had managed to offend someone. I remember one incident in Oklahoma City at a bar called the Esquire

Lounge, which we frequented on weekends. Two guys who looked as if they could play linebacker in the National Football League got into an argument over a woman and decided to take their differences outside to the parking lot. As they shed their jackets Pat suggested not too tactfully to the smaller of the two, whom I conservatively estimated to weigh about two hundred and twenty pounds, that he was going to get killed by the bigger guy. Of course Pat did it in a voice loud enough for the few remaining patrons in the bar to hear him. Naturally the guy took offense at having his physical ability challenged and announced he would warm up for the main event by whipping Pat's "skinny butt." Somehow I managed to convince him that beating up someone whom he outweighed by a good hundred pounds was really not a good way to prove his manhood. Somewhat reluctantly he agreed and turned his attention to his antagonist who was already stripped to the waist and showing arms the size of my thighs. I didn't say anything but I suspected Pat was right in his assessment of the guy's chances. I managed to quietly steer Pat to the safety of the car and headed home to the safety of our small apartment before he insulted someone else.

Fred Gilligan had a beer gut and a handshake to match his shoulders. His face bore the scars of many a fight. One particularly ugly one extended from his right temple down his cheek and across his chin. Even the week's growth of whiskers he wore couldn't hide it. I wondered what the other guy must have looked like after the fight.

"Bottle of Coors," I said to the old man behind the bar. He was wearing a St. Louis baseball cap and a filthy apron that he alternately used to dry his hands, wipe the bar and dry glasses with. He brought the beer, but not a glass. I didn't mind, especially after watching him use his apron.

"What took you so long?" Pat wanted to know. "We've been sitting here for almost an hour."

"I can tell that," I said, waving to the several empty beer bottles that sat in front of them.

"Hey, Fred," Pat said, "how about giving my friend a ride too? Won't be crowded and he's good company."

"Sure, I reckon so," the old man replied. With that he chugged the new bottle the barkeep had just set down and announced that it was time to go.

"Tell you what," Pat said, "We'll buy the beer, as long as we're riding free." All the beer was making Pat uncharacteristically generous. Cheap was also another one of Pat's traits. In our circle of friends he was always the last to come up with his share of beer or gas money for our weekend excursions to Oklahoma City's bars and clubs.

I looked at Fred's enormous gut and thought maybe it would have been cheaper to take the bus. *What the hell though*, I thought. *It's still better than riding a smelly bus or train.* I ordered two six packs and told the barkeep to throw in a church key.

Pat and Fred got in the front seat and I got in the back with the beer. I popped a can for each of us. Fred turned the motor over and it sounded great for a '39 Chevy. He must have been a good mechanic for the Chevy ran like a new Harley, hardly making any noise at all. Fred seemed to know just how to coax the most out of it. Fred Gilligan was a rover, I quickly discovered. He had retired from the Navy after twenty years and had held several jobs since that time. It wasn't that he didn't like the jobs he took; it was that he just didn't like to stay in one place very long. Since his retirement, he had been a policeman in Sacramento for a few years and a long distance truck driver after that stint. He was just now coming back from working for 18 months on an offshore oilrig in the Gulf. Now he was headed for California to see what he could do. I was quickly discovering that one thing he could do was drink a lot of beer. Whoever wrote the propaganda for Alcoholics Anonymous, about drinking and driving, never met Fred Gilligan. He seemed to drink about a beer a mile, for we had hardly started before we were into the second six-pack.

After about thirty minutes we needed to take a piss stop. We were also out of Coors. There was a little town right off the main road where we could take care of both needs.

Bucklin, Kansas, was certainly a place I would hate to get stranded in for any length of time. Like so many of the small towns in rural

Kansas and Nebraska, it was a sad little place. The focus of activity as always in small towns is centered around the school, church and local cafe. It had a main street two or three blocks long with a few decaying buildings on either side. Several of them were boarded up and none seemed to be doing any business. In contrast to all of this, was the cafe-gas station-convenience store at the end of Main Street, which appeared to be doing a booming business. The gravel parking lot was filled with pickup trucks. Most of them were covered with a month's worth of dust and mud. They all sported huge toolboxes and sacks of cattle feed in their beds, along with assorted dents to the vehicles themselves.

Inside the cafe a dozen farmers sat at Formica tables sipping coffee and large glasses of iced tea. The uniform of Bucklin seemed to be either Round House overalls or Levi jeans. All of the men wore baseball type caps emblazoned with the logo of insurance agencies or farm implement dealers. They eyed us as if they though we might be fugitives on the run from the FBI.

When Fred asked the overweight cashier if we could buy beer she pointed a thick finger in the direction of the convenience store and announced in a shrill voice: "Got to buy your liquor over there, we don't serve no alcohol in this cafe."

After relieving ourselves in the gas station restroom and picking up a case of Coors, we left Bucklin just as the sun was vanishing over the flat Kansas horizon.

Fred was beginning to feel the effects of the twelve or so beers he had drunk. Pat had long since felt the effects and curled up in the corner of the front seat with a bottle of Coors still in his hand. While the beer might have loosened Fred's tongue, it sure as hell didn't affect his driving. If anything, the old Chevy seemed to respond like it was on automatic pilot. The beer flowed as easily as the time and the miles passed quickly.

With Pat asleep in the corner, Fred began to talk about his days in the Navy. He recounted his time on ships during the Korean War and how he would have liked to have seen more action. He wondered about the escalating conflict in Southeast Asia and predicted that I would be spending time over there before long. That was a thought that didn't bring a lot of comfort to me, but I was interested in hearing what he had to say about the situation. His comments brought back memories of my last ROTC drill at the university just a few days earlier. A few protestors stationed themselves on the drill field with placards denouncing the war in Vietnam and President Kennedy in particular. I had to admit that at the time I really didn't think much about what was happening but I was surprised to learn that some people already thought of our actions as an act of war. Frankly I was a little confused as to just what the protestors were complaining about. Fred's comments gave me a little more to think about.

I discovered that Fred was more than just a rover; he was opinionated and very intelligent. He cursed the British and the French for letting the world situation get to where it was. He believed if they had stood up to Hitler and Mussolini earlier there would not have been a second war. He particularly hated the French, calling them a "bunch of limp wrist pansies who always depended on someone else to bail them out of trouble." He also gave plenty of blame to the United States for not being more forceful with Russia after the war. He though Truman was right for dropping the bomb, but cursed him for dismissing MacArthur. He sounded so much like my grandfather I found myself getting nostalgic. He had absolutely no kind words for President Kennedy, whom he characterized as a skirt chaser who would make a pact with the devil as long as he could be president. I couldn't help but think that if my history professor had been as interesting as Fred I might have paid more attention.

I also discovered that he had a bit of the romantic in him, as his voice became gentler when he spoke of his ex-wife and his son. She had left him during the Korean War, taking their two-year-old boy. He didn't blame her, however, saying that the military was no place for a man with a family. She lived somewhere in Wisconsin with her new husband and the child. He never told me if he visited his son, but I could tell by the way he spoke of him that he would like to. I tried to imagine what it would be like to have a son and not ever talk to him or see him. I suppose there are some things in life that are more painful than being separated from those we love, although at the moment I could not think of any.

For most of the rest of the time together we rode in silence. Fred and I drank the last of the beer while Pat, who was now stretched out in the back seat snored quietly. We stopped twice to relieve ourselves by the side of the road and I wondered if there was anyplace in the world that had more stars in the sky than a clear Kansas night. Just looking at them made me think of my last high school prom. A blue ceiling adorned with hundreds of glittering paper stars and a beautiful girl dancing slowly in my arms was an image that suddenly came to my mind. For a moment I swear I could smell her perfume wafting over the soft prairie wind. Then it was gone, just as she was. When we reached Walsenburg, Colorado, the next day Fred pulled the Chevy into a Texaco station for gas and we all got out. He was taking Highway 160 west to California and another adventure. We were heading north towards Denver.

While Fred filled the Chevy with gas, we bought him a six-pack as a farewell gift. In his generous way, he insisted that we have a bottle before he left. So we sat on cases of oil and drank the beer while the surly attendant gave us nasty looks and muttered something unintelligible.

I really hated to see old Fred leave. I have often wondered whatever became of him and even now I can remember everything about his grizzled face and the old black Chevy. Probably of all the people I have met in the years since, Fred is the one who seemed to know how to enjoy life the most. I hope that he made it back to see his son. It would be a shame not to know a father like him.

We finished our beers and threw the empty bottles in a fifty-five-gallon barrel by the grease racks. While Fred roared off in a shower of gravel, Pat pulled a quarter from his pocket for the toss to see who would go ahead. This time I lost the coin toss, so I picked up my bag and started walking. The attendant at the station had told me to stay on the road and keep walking for about a mile and then I would be on the edge of the city and should be able to catch a ride. After about fifteen minutes of walking, I dropped my bag and stuck out my thumb.

Pat and I had agreed that we would meet in Colorado Springs that afternoon if we didn't meet on the road again. As it turned out, I wouldn't see Pat again until we reached Strasborg.

The land between Walsenburg and Colorado Springs is mostly flat, with vast stretches of semi-arid land that was home to a few cattle and horses. Occasionally a ranch or farm house dotted the landscape with wispy clouds of smoke coming from their chimney. Even though it was early June, it was cold in Colorado. In the background the Rockies still sported a cap of snow. I wondered why people lived out here and how they could make a living in such a desolate place. When I thought about it some more I realized that the people here were probably not that much different than those who lived on the farms and ranches where I grew up in Oklahoma. It seemed apparent that the big difference was the size of the ranches and the distance between home sites. I had not seen a human being or car since I had left the gas station. I was getting a little nervous since the sun was about to set. I was not looking forward to the prospect of spending the night on the side of the road in such a desolate and lonely place. I could imagine wolves and grizzly bears roaming the hills, even though neither one had been seen in Colorado in probably the last fifty years.

Finally I saw a car approaching from the direction of Walsenburg. In the distance it was only a small dot on the highway but I dropped my bag hoping that the driver would be sympathetic and give me a ride. As the dot grew larger I could see that it was a Volkswagon and I almost decided not to stick out my thumb. Experience had taught me that few small cars stop for riders for obvious reasons. As the Bug got closer I could see that the driver was the only occupant so I turned to face it and threw out my hand. To my surprise the little car began to slow down and pulled up to a stop beside me. I opened the door, threw my bag in the cramped quarters and crawled in the passenger seat. I was astonished to discover the driver was a beautiful girl about my age.

"Where are you going?" she asked.

"All the way to Washington," I answered, trying not to stare at her.

"I can take you as far as Denver, that's where I'm going," she said.

"That's great. I really appreciate you stopping for me."

"No problem," she said, shifting the Volkswagon into gear and pulling back on to the highway.

Her name was Leigh and she was beautiful. She was also rich, which always helps. To be more precise, her father was rich. He was big in cement in Dallas and his only daughter could have anything she wanted. The funny thing was, she didn't want much of anything. She could have been driving a Jag or Corvette, but she had a four-year-old Volkswagen. She could have stayed in Dallas and attended the debutante ball, but she was going to Denver to work in a day care center for low-income kids. When I asked her why Denver and not Dallas, she explained that it had something to do with college and community service. Besides, she wanted out of Dallas for the summer.

She was easy to talk to and had volunteered most of the information about herself and family in the first fifteen minutes. I kept sneaking looks at her by pretending that I was adjusting myself in the small front seat. I was sure that she was aware of what I was doing but I couldn't help myself.

She had long hair as black as any I have ever seen on a woman. It came down to the middle of her shoulder blades but it curled up at the end. I was glad she was not wearing it straight and looking as if it had been ironed, which was becoming a popular fad at the time with a lot of girls. She was fairly tall, I guessed around five-foot-eight, but it was hard to tell in the tight quarters of the little car. Even though I couldn't really see her eyes in the semi-darkness, I somehow knew they were the same color as her hair. I was almost right. She gripped the steering wheel with long slender fingers that had only a hint of clear polish on her well-manicured nails. I knew she would probably slap my face for what I was thinking. I also knew it would be worth it.

The Bug rolled through the late evening as the sun played its magic on the Colorado flatlands. Just as the sun began to dip below the horizon bright steaks of blue and orange made zigzag patterns across the almost dark sky. For just a moment the sun's rays illuminated the interior of the little car and I took the opportunity to look more closely at her. I wasn't disappointed in what I saw. It's funny how a person can always associate certain characteristics with particular states. I had always thought Colorado was nothing more than the snow-capped Rockies and Pike's Peak, so I was really surprised after we had crossed over into Colorado with Fred and had traveled for miles before seeing anything that could be called a mountain. I thought of my own state of Oklahoma and how many people had formed their opinion of it as a dust bowl wasteland based on the novel *The Grapes of Wrath*. The truth is that Sallisaw, Oklahoma, the town the Joad family came from in Steinbeck's book, is in eastern Oklahoma. That part of the state is heavily wooded with numerous lakes and rivers, totally unlike the flatlands of the Panhandle.

I got my mind off geography as Leigh and I continued to get better acquainted. She was a junior at Southern Methodist University. She agreed to attend school there as a concession to her father, who evidently had some misgivings about his daughter's values and lifestyle. She never spoke harshly of him, but only said that they had different values in life. He wanted to make money and she wanted to make friends. I wondered if the two were mutually exclusive.

She told me she was an elementary education major and hoped to work in either a low-income school or perhaps start her own day care center after she graduated. Whatever she did, she was adamant that it would not be in Dallas. I asked her what was wrong with Dallas.

"Too many fakes," she smiled at me, showing the most perfect and whitest teeth I had ever seen. "Everyone in my crowd thinks you measure success by how many dresses you have from Neiman Marcus. That's okay for them, but I would rather work in charity than give to charity balls," she said. I wondered for a moment if her father's wealth had made her so naïve that it had clouded her judgment of the real world. I quickly dismissed the thought, as she seemed too sincere in what she was saying.

She admitted the job in Denver was her first time away from home for any length of time and that she was nervous about traveling alone.

I asked her if she knew it wasn't smart to pick up hitchhikers.

"I know," she said softly. "Daddy warned me, but you looked so lonely standing there. Besides, I don't like to drive alone at night."

I was amazed at her innocence but somehow touched by her commitment to her beliefs. She really believed that she could make a difference in the world and she was determined to try. I found myself believing that if anyone could, she would be able to do it.

I was so engrossed in our conversation that I hadn't even realized the sun had set a long time ago. I suddenly found myself wishing that she was going a lot farther than Denver.

The little car seemed to huff and puff as we approached Pueblo, as the altitude seemed to be taking its toll. At times we were hardly going forty miles an hour. I was sure the carburetor was not adjusted for the mountains of Colorado and I began to wonder if we would make it to Denver.

Pueblo is a steel mill town and as we approached it I saw what at first sight looked like low lying, puffy, white clouds. As we rolled into the edge of the city I realized that they were columns of smoke and steam from the mills. I knew that steel mills never shut their furnaces down because it takes too much energy and time to get them fired up again. I thought to myself what a shame it was the people living there probably never got to see the real beauty of the place. The constant belching of the smoke and steam from the smoke towers made that unlikely.

Even in the darkness I could see that the houses and cars all seemed to be covered in a dirty gray film. The street lights did little to brighten the dreary, depressing scene of small, frame homes. Most of them seemed to have at least one rusty broken down automobile setting in the yard.

I was glad when we reached the north edge of the city where things seemed to be cleaner. I rolled the window down, hoping to get a breath of fresh air and was jolted by what smelled like burning rubber. I wondered if people in Pueblo ever got used to the smell and the grime or if they simply looked at it as what they had to contend with in order to make a living. Most of them were probably no different than my own father, who seemed to accept whatever life dealt him as simply his lot in life without anything he could do about it. I knew for sure that I did not want to live my life with such a helpless feeling.

Leigh decided that we had enough gas to get to Colorado Springs, so we picked up speed as we left the city limits and began the drive north to Denver. The Volkswagen continued to labor hard and I thought I could hear a suspicious sound coming from the engine. I told Leigh that maybe we should have it checked when we got to Colorado Springs. She surprised me by saying that it was probably just the carburetor not being adjusted to the high altitude. I wondered where rich girls from Dallas learned about adjusting carburetors.

The distance from Pueblo to Colorado Springs is only about fifty miles, but the way the Bug was running and sputtering it took us over an hour and a half to get there. I certainly didn't mind because I was not looking forward to leaving Leigh's company.

We filled the time by telling each other more about ourselves. Although I wanted to know all about her, she kept turning the questions back to me. She insisted that her life was quite boring and ordinary. Her parents had sent her to private schools all her life, since according to her father, "the public schools just don't measure up." She had done all the usual things, including being a cheerleader for two years but never enjoying it, she confessed. It was just something that her parents expected her to do, as she explained it. It was obvious that while she was willing to be guided by her parents, she was not going to be controlled by them.

She was fascinated that I had grown up living in the country. One of her dreams she confided was to own a ranch, where she could bring underprivileged kids for the summer. She admitted that she had never been on a ranch despite the notion that most people had of all Texans owning thousands of acres with an oil well on each one.

When we pulled into Colorado Springs I suggested that we stop at a Conoco station that advertised "Mechanic on duty 24 hours a day." Since no other cars were present she pulled the Bug into the bay area of the station and killed the engine. A sleepy eyed attendant came out carrying a copy of some sort of hot rod magazine and drinking a Dr.

Pepper. I didn't see anyone else around so I assumed that he must be the mechanic who obviously doubled as the night manager.

"Help you?" he wanted to know, looking at Leigh all the time. I don't believe he knew anyone else was in the car until I spoke.

"I was wondering if your mechanic could take a look at the carburetor," I said. "I think it might need a little adjustment since we are coming from Dallas and I don't think it's tuned for this altitude."

"Sure thing," he said. "Happens all the time up here. People come up on vacation from the flatlands and forget that their cars are just like their bodies. The altitude takes some getting used to so they have to be fine tuned a little bit."

"How long do you think it will take?" Leigh asked.

"Well, if that's all it is, shouldn't take long at all. You in a real big hurry?"

"Not at all," she replied. "Is there a cafe close by where we could get a cup of coffee?"

"Just over there at the motel." He pointed in the direction that indicated the motel was somewhere behind the building.

"Thanks," I said. "Why don't you take a look at it and we'll be back in a half hour or so."

"Sure thing," he answered, opening the door and turning over the engine so he could listen to the motor.

The motel was one of those small units with about a dozen rooms that catered to truckers. It was a low-slung concrete building of dirty orange with an asphalt roof. I imagined to tired truckers it looked like an oasis after six days on the road. The cafe was vintage truck stop, complete with a skinny, blond waitress in a beehive hairdo. She was serving up large plates of steak and eggs, hamburgers and fries with hot coffee to half a dozen truckers. We slid into a yellow vinyl plastic booth that had a large rip in the middle of it that someone had attempted to repair with duct tape. I motioned for the waitress.

"What'll it be?" the skinny blonde asked, with an accent that I thought sounded like west Texas drawl.

"Two coffees," I said, looking at Leigh to make sure that was all she wanted. She indicated that was ok with her and excused herself to go to the ladies room.

She got back to the booth at the same time the coffee arrived. Picking up the steaming cup, she blew tentatively on the hot liquid and looked at me over the top of it.

"So tell me more about what it's like to live in the country," she asked.

"Not much to tell," I answered. "You miss a lot of things that your friends do because you live so far out and it's a real pain to have to drive that far into town to do anything. There's a lot of work that always needs to be done and nobody ever comes to see you because it's too far. I don't think you would like it."

"I think I would like it just fine." She smiled and sipped her coffee.

"Why are you going all the way to Washington to work this summer?" She was suddenly full of questions.

"Because I'm tired of riding the rodeo the way I have for the last two summers. There has to be an easier way to make enough money for college. And besides, I wanted to see some country other than Oklahoma."

"You ride in rodeos?" she said, setting her coffee down with a thump and sloshing a little on the tabletop.

"Just the small town ones in the summer."

"You mean like with horses and bulls and all of that kind of thing?" She was looking at me as if I had just confessed to being Jack the Ripper.

"Well," I admitted, somewhat tentatively, "that's what you generally find in most rodeos."

She was staring into her coffee and I had a feeling I wasn't going to like what she was thinking. People who are generally so sympathetic and caring for children feel the same way about animals. I had discovered this fact a long time ago.

"But it must hurt them terribly," she said, in a voice that seemed tinged with more sadness than disapproval.

"How many rodeos have you been too?" I asked.

"None, I don't approve of them," she replied, flipping her long black hair back and setting back in the booth.

"Well then how do you know how the animals are treated?" I hoped that I wasn't taking a defensive position that perhaps couldn't stand up to her convictions.

She was giving me a look that said, "Don't get me started on this or you will regret it." Foolishly, I plunged ahead, knowing full well that I was not going to change her mind.

"Look," I said, "does it make sense that the owners of the stock would allow them to be mistreated? These animals are valuable property and expensive to replace. Some of the horses are almost fifteen years old. They really have a pretty good life and are well taken care of. I've never seen one hurt yet in the two years I have been riding." I looked for some small sign of acceptance in her face but I could tell she was unmoved by my logic.

She was making small circular motions with her coffee cup, creating wet rings on the Formica table top while staring at me with eyes so blue they were almost black. I hoped she wasn't going to tell me to walk the rest of the way to Denver.

"How about you?" she asked. "Have you ever been hurt?"

"Only once, when I got careless and a bull stepped on me and bruised some ribs."

"Well, it probably served you right," she said, raising her eyebrows and giving me a little smile. I took her response as a degree of forgiveness, if not acceptance of my sin. I decided to change the subject while I could.

"Your car may be ready by now," I said, picking up the check the waitress had left. "Why don't we go check on it."?

The mechanic was just finishing when we arrived and announced that the Bug was ready. He explained that it was indeed just an adjustment that needed to be made for the altitude and that it shouldn't cause any more problems. "Cars are just like humans," he announced, "they take a little more oxygen up here than in the flatlands."

Leigh asked him how much she owed and he thought for a few seconds before saying, "Six bucks ought to cover it." He slid the bills into the pocket of his greasy coveralls and I wondered how many repairs never got reported to the owner of the gas station.

The distance from Colorado Springs to Denver is only about sixty miles and Leigh continued to ask me questions about what it was like living in the country and such a small town. I really didn't mind because I could tell she was genuinely interested and I found that a bit flattering. I couldn't imagine what she thought was so interesting about my life and boring about hers. I could think of a lot of girls that I went to school with that would have traded places with her in an instant. Somehow it made me a little sad to think of such a beautiful, rich girl who was obviously so discontented with her life. I was a little ashamed of myself for wondering if she would still find her life so unacceptable after working a summer with low income kids.

True to the gas station attendant's promise, the Volkswagen ran like a new one all the way to Denver. A huge billboard welcoming us to the Mile High City of Denver about two o'clock in the morning greeted us. The lights of the city were beautiful as they reflected off what I knew to be the Rockies still some distance away. I had long ago forgotten my promise to meet Pat in Colorado Springs.

"Hungry?" Leigh asked.

"Yes," I answered, eager for any chance to extend the time I had with her.

"Good, let's find a diner and get some breakfast," she suggested.

Folger's Diner, on Colfax Avenue in downtown Denver, is one of those all-night places where at three o'clock in the morning you can count on being served the best breakfast you have ever eaten. At that time of the morning the late night crowd had pretty well cleared out and it would be another couple of hours before the early workers arrived. The place was deserted, except for a couple of truckers who were too intent on working on their steak and eggs to pay much attention to anyone.

On the way in we saw a couple of winos sharing a bottle from a brown paper bag and I realized why Colfax was a familiar name to me. I remembered that this was the place where Jack Kerouac and his group of crazies had spent a lot of time. He had written about Folger's Diner during the late Forties and early Fifties, when he was hitchhiking across the country. It didn't look as if the place had changed much since then.

We took a back booth, far from the jukebox where I recognized Bobby Bare, singing about being five hundred miles from home. That wasn't quite as far as I was at the moment.

I like girls who have a healthy appetite and Leigh had a great one. I had already learned that women who enjoy food usually enjoy everything else in life. We ordered the same thing: two eggs scrambled, hash browns, bacon, toast and black coffee.

The cook was either being wasted in a place like Folgers or he put extra care into his breakfasts. The waitress brought two mugs of coffee, slopping a little on the table as she set them down. I forgave her since she looked to be pushing seventy.

The coffee was good and we were ready for seconds when our breakfast arrived. The eggs were just right——mountains of yellow with a hint of butter. The bacon was crisp, not greasy, and the hash browns crunchy and made from fresh potatoes. We concentrated on the breakfast.

The waitress brought the check with our third cup of coffee and I took it while Leigh smiled and said, "You really don't have to be so gallant. I can pay for my own."

"It's the least I can do," I muttered. "Besides, I'm not paying for the ride, you know."

"Would it make you feel better if you were?" she asked.

"Probably," I answered. "I'm just funny that way."

She laughed a deep throaty laugh and took my hand. "Spoken like a true gentleman, but it really isn't necessary. Besides, I've enjoyed your company. I felt much safer having you with me."

She let her fingers linger on the back of my hand and then announced, "Time to go, but I need to visit the bathroom first. I'll be right back."

While she was gone I finished my coffee and thought about how incredibly lucky I was to have caught a ride that would take me all the way to Denver.

She returned in a few minutes and I was surprised to see that she had combed her hair and put on fresh lipstick. She looked even more beautiful in the bright lights of the diner. The white sweater and dark slacks she was wearing did nothing to hide her shapely figure. I noticed that the truckers were paying more attention to her than their breakfast now.

It was almost four a.m. and I wasn't sure what the next move would be. We both got into the Bug and she backed out and headed west on Colfax. I assumed she was planning to take me to the highway on the edge of town, where I might have a chance of picking up a ride from someone headed over the Rockies, maybe even to Salt Lake City. Colfax was coming alive with the early morning workers. People were going home from the night shift, bums came stumbling from the alleys where they had spent the night, poking in the refuse of last night's garbage, hoping to find the last dregs from a bottle of whiskey or wine. The street itself was lined with cheap, seedy motels. Neon signs beckoned the weary traveler or the whores who brought their customers in for thirty minutes of hollow passion. Love by the hour or half hour in a rented bed. I wondered what their lives were like and suddenly felt very depressed and lonely. I knew it wasn't just the dirt and grime of Colfax that was making me feel that way. It was the hopelessness I saw in the faces of the people and I wondered how far away I was from becoming one of them. For two years I had wallowed in my own misery, unable or unwilling to do anything about it except to drink so much that the friends I had left were beginning to worry about me. As I looked at the men and women on Colfax Avenue I wondered how many of them were here now because like me, they had mistakenly believed that just loving someone would always be enough. Love, I had discovered was never just enough.

When the chance came for me to actually take the job in Strasborg for the summer I jumped at it. I didn't do it for the money, because I knew I could probably make more money by riding the rodeo circuit or working construction. I was hoping that the distance between my hometown and Strasborg would help erase some of the memories of the last two years.

Colfax Avenue claims to be the longest street in the United States. I believed it since we had been driving for at least half an hour before we reached the main highway that would carry me over the Rockies and into Utah. I realized how tired I was and was thinking that Leigh must be exhausted also. Suddenly, she pulled the Bug off the road onto an access ramp and into the parking lot of a motel. She switched off the ignition and turned to face me.

"Look," she said, "we're both tired and you can't catch a ride at this hour, so let's check in here and get some rest. I don't have to report until day after tomorrow and you can get started tomorrow, after you've gotten some sleep."

If she though I was going to object, she was wrong. "Okay with me," I said, as I opened the door and reached for my bag.

She was still sitting behind the wheel. All of a sudden my hands were sweating and I wasn't sleepy anymore. "I'll be right back," I said, not knowing what else to say or do.

"Hey," she called after me, "if you get a single, it'll be cheaper." I was sure she was smiling when she said that.

Now, I had been with girls before, but this was the first time I had been taken to a motel by a girl I had only known a few hours. I filled out the card with a shaky hand and handed it to the kid behind the desk.

"You forgot your license number," he said, around the toothpick in his mouth.

"I don't know it," I said quietly.

He shifted the toothpick but never looked up, just handed me the key.

We found our room, the last one at the end of the small unit. I tried not to show my nervousness as I fumbled with the key to the door. It wasn't much of a room, only a single bed, dresser, two nightstands and lamps with their shades slightly askew. A large watercolor of the Rocky Mountains hung over the headboard. Elk grazed in a pasture by a clear stream but I really wasn't interested in the picture. I dropped the bags near the dresser and Leigh picked up one of hers, then excused herself to go to the bathroom.

I turned off the lights in the room except for the one on the nightstand by the side of the bed where I stretched out after taking off my boots. Leigh seemed to be taking a long time in the bathroom so

I undressed and crawled between the sheets, which were cool and soft on my bare skin. Suddenly I was very tired.

The door to the bathroom opened and Leigh came out. I could see that she had no makeup on, which went perfectly with everything else she was wearing. I opened the covers for her as neither one of us said a word. She slipped her lean, tanned body in next to mine and nestled her head into my shoulder. I could feel the strength of the long, hard muscles in her back as I pulled her to me and I guessed they came from playing tennis. At the high school I had attended we didn't have one single girl's sport offered, so my contact with female athletes was rather limited. I closed my eyes and imagined her dressed in tennis whites, long brown legs racing back and forth across a tennis court, smashing the ball to a tired opponent. I liked the idea that she might be involved in something so physical and competitive.

"Time to get some sleep," she murmured, laying her open palm across my chest.

I turned out the light and felt her long fingernails tracing the outline of my chin. I wished that I had shaved, but I was not about to do it at that moment.

I awoke to the sound of running water. Leigh came out of the bathroom pulling a brush through her long black hair. The towel she had wrapped around her only accentuated her beautiful body. I rolled over onto her pillow and breathed deeply. The smell of her hair and perfume was still in the pillow and brought back the memory of a few hours ago.

"Better get up," she said, just like she was placing an order for breakfast. "It's almost five," she noted, tapping her watch. "That's five p.m.," she said, as I showed no interest in moving.

"You've been sleeping since four this morning."

"As I remember, I didn't get right to sleep," I corrected her.

She flashed that smile and threw me the towel she was wearing. Utah would have to wait.

An hour later I slipped out of the bed and headed for the bathroom. Fifteen minutes later, I was showered, shaved and into a clean set of clothes and feeling great, except for the fact I realized we were nearing the end of what had been a very special time.

We parted company over a cup of coffee in a cafe across the street. We made small talk and vague promises to look each other up if I came back through Denver or if she was ever in Oklahoma. We both knew it would never happen.

We kissed goodbye in front of her Volkswagen. Without another word; I started walking towards the access road, which led to the highway some hundred yards away. When I reached the top of the hill, I turned to look at the place I had left her. The Volkswagen was gone, but I had enough memories to last for the rest of the trip.

I've met a lot of girls since Leigh, but none came into my life and left such an impression in such a short time as she did. It wasn't just the night we spent together. It was the timing. I suppose the word for it today would be serendipity. Some might call it just plain good luck, but it was more than that. It was two people, frightened by being alone in a different world who for a few brief hours took refuge in each other and found solace and comfort. I know plenty of people who would condemn us for that night, if not sentencing us to a hell they are so certain exists. Such people I generally discover to have secrets of their own. Secrets when uncovered usually expose a hypocrite rather than a saint.

I often thought about going back and looking her up again, but something always kept me from it. Maybe the thought that the second time would not be like I remembered the first. Or perhaps there wouldn't be a second time at all. Maybe we would rather have our memories and the way we want things to be, rather than face the possibility that it never was like we thought at all.

CHAPTER II

I didn't have long to wait for a ride once I reached the main highway. A green Ford slowed, and then came to a stop about five minutes after I got there. The driver was a small, thin man of about sixty-five with a neatly trimmed gray mustache. His name was Harry Moore and he was a map salesman. Actually, he sold atlases, which I found out were not really maps at all. He didn't like the term "map" when talking about atlases. I could see he was a man who took pride in his work and I like to see that in people. He had worked for the same company since 1936 and sold mainly to schools and large libraries.

After he corrected me for calling his atlases maps, and gave me a twenty-minute explanation of the differences in the two, he went on to tell me about the Great Depression he had lived through and how the government today was ripping off young people. It was a lecture I had heard many times before from my father and his relatives.

"Take for instance, your social security you're going to pay this summer," he said, poking his finger towards the windshield. "You know you won't ever get a penny of that money back, don't you?" he asked.

"No, why not?" I answered him, just to be polite.

"Well, because there won't be any by the time you're sixty-five and want to retire." He stated this as if it was such an obvious truth that I felt pretty dumb, just asking why.

"You see," he went on, obviously thrilled to have a captive audience, "there's no such thing as a social security fund at all. Every cent you pay just goes into the treasury and then it goes out in welfare, the wars, salaries for crooked politicians and everything else." I could see I was in for a speech he had given many times before and probably never tired of telling.

"Oh, I see," I answered, not really seeing anything at all. I was hopeful that he would be satisfied and move on to another topic of conversation. I was not going to be so lucky.

"Look," he said, with a touch of exasperation in his voice, "you know what a deficit is, don't you?"

"Yes, I know what a deficit is," I volunteered. I was thankful for Economics 103 and the C grade I had managed to pull.

"Well," he went right on talking, "a deficit is when you pay out more than you take in."

Apparently he didn't believe I knew anything about economics or deficits as he continued his discourse.

"You see, each year the government pays out more than it takes in, so there's a deficit. That means the money you pay in now is going to someone who has already retired and is drawing your money." He was looking at me with a look that clearly said: "Surely any idiot can understand something this simple."

I didn't know much about economics, but I didn't like the idea of paying for someone else's retirement.

"Look, if I'm paying for old people's social security now, why can't someone pay for mine when I'm old?" I challenged him with what I thought was perfectly good logic.

"No, no," he insisted, aware now that he had an idiot on his hands when it came to understanding how the government worked. "The deficit will be too big by then, don't you see? It doesn't work that way," he replied softly, more to himself I thought than to me. Then he grew quiet for the first time since picking me up.

Since I wanted to change the subject I asked him why he didn't retire.

"Oh, I'm old enough," he said. "Retirement isn't good for people as long as they can work. As soon as a person retires all he does is sit in his rocking chair and pretty soon he's dead from boredom. Give a man a good honest day's work and he has something to live for. Remember that when you start your own work," he advised me with a waggle of his finger.

Actually, I was tired of discussing what was wrong with the government and wanted to just relax and take in the mountain scenery. Since it was summer, I still had a couple of hours to enjoy the mountains and the shadows the evening sun was playing on them before nightfall.

We headed west and soon were passing signs indicating towns like Georgetown and Evergreen. Not far out of Denver, we passed a sign that indicated the grave of Buffalo Bill. I wondered how old Bill would like his mountains, now that they were being bulldozed to make way for superhighways that would carry passengers all the way from Denver to Salt Lake without stopping, except to fill up with gasoline. However, when I thought about it, old Bill was not exactly a conservationist. He almost single handedly exterminated the buffalo population.

The scenery from Denver to Salt Lake City has to be some of the most beautiful anywhere. I wished that Mr. Moore would take a little time and enjoy the scenic overlooks advertised along the roadway but I could tell he was in a hurry to get home. It was getting close to sundown now and the sun and shadows were doing fantastic things to the mountains. I was sorry I was going over the Rockies at night, because I didn't want to miss anything. As things turned out, there was a full moon and I could see almost as well as if it had been daylight.

The old man had not said anything for quite a while and I began to wonder if he was getting sleepy. Riding over the Rockies can be a scary thing with a good driver, but when it is with a sixty-five-year-old the ride gets even scarier.

"If you want me to drive a while, I'll be glad to," I offered, trying to sound casual.

Mr. Moore laughed loudly and I knew he had been reading my mind.

"I've been driving these mountains since 1936, kid. You don't have to worry about me going to sleep on you, although I could probably drive them asleep. If I get tired, I'll let you know."

I was embarrassed for my mistake, so I didn't say anything else. Anyway, he was right. He knew these roads probably as well as anyone and we seemed to glide over the mountains and around the curves as if we were on rails.

The ride helped me understand why some people fall in love with the mountains so easily. I was unprepared for their enormous size and at times felt claustrophobic because they seemed to push in on me. At the summit of each pass we were treated to a spectacular scene of miles of valleys carpeted in aspen, evergreen and pine. Each new curve in the road brought more of the same and I knew why people lived in those places. Unfortunately, even though we were enjoying a full moon, I knew the mountains would be even more incredible in the full daylight. The only thing I didn't like was the snow. Although it was early June, the snow was still on the roadside. It was interesting to watch the road signs, which depicted the various curves, bends and dips in the road. One was just a question mark, which I thought at least showed some originality and humor.

Mr. Moore seemed to pay no attention to the scenery and I suppose that he had come to take it for granted since he had been traveling these same highways for over twenty-five years. For a flatlander like myself it was an exhilarating experience and I knew I wanted to come back for a closer and longer look at the Rockies.

"Hungry?" he suddenly interrupted my thoughts.

"Yes, I guess I am." I realized the last time I had eaten was the breakfast with Leigh. That had been at four o'clock that morning and it was now almost nine at night. The thought of Leigh saddened me, as I remembered the events of the previous day and night. The few hours I had spent with her now seemed to be more of a dream than reality. For a moment I found myself wishing that I had gotten a phone number or the name of the day care center so I could call or write her. I knew however, that what had happened between the two of us would never happen again so I had to be content with my memories.

Vail, Colorado, is nestled snugly into the mountains about eighty miles from Denver and is the favorite destination of thousand of skiers and more than a few movie stars. We arrived shortly after nine o'clock and Mr. Moore pulled into a spot in front of the lodge. It was a beautiful building made from rough logs, cedar, stone and glass. We went through the sliding glass doors into the huge lobby with a cathedral ceiling and an enormous fireplace, which occupied one wall.

We walked up stone steps and into a bar that looked as if it had come right out of a western magazine. The bar was nice but the view provided was even better. An enclosed swimming pool stood on the other side of a set of sliding glass doors. Three bikini clad women cavorted around the edges laughing and splashing water at each other with their shapely legs. They made a striking contrast to the snow that covered the ground outside.

We decided to eat in the dining room and chose a spot that would give us a full view of the pool and the bikinis.

Mr. Moore recommended the trout and I was glad he did. Although I'm not a fish lover, this was light, tender, and flaky. The waiter assured me that it was caught fresh that morning. I've never eaten any fish like it since, including the ones I have caught myself. We washed it all down with Coors beer, which has its brewery in Golden, near Denver.

After I finished the trout, I excused myself while Mr. Moore had his coffee. I wanted to get a closer look at the bar and the scenery around the pool.

There was a rancher and his girlfriend occupying a corner table, another middle-aged couple finishing their dinner and three young guys sitting on bar stools near the fireplace. A folk singer was singing about the wreck of the old Ninety-Seven and the way he sang it, you would have thought he was on that locomotive when it jumped the tracks. It was an old Hank Snow tune that I had heard many times while growing up in Oklahoma.

I sat down on one of the tall stools at the bar and the bartender, a young guy with a great handlebar mustache, came up to take my order. I asked for a draft beer and when he took my five he only brought back three ones. I was used to buying a whole six-pack for a dollar and a half. I began to realize how they could afford indoor pools and fireplaces. The folk singer finished the wreck just as Mr. Moore came in and ordered a brandy. We listened to a couple more songs, then decided we had better be on the road again.

The night was really beautiful. A huge, full, yellow moon hung over the mountains casting enough light to make the street lamps unnecessary. I could smell wood smoke from the fireplace in the lodge and pulled my light windbreaker closer as I realized just how cold it could be in the mountains in June.

We got into the car and Mr. Moore turned on the heater to take away the chill that had settled in it while we were having dinner. He seemed to be lost in his own thoughts and talked little for the rest of the trip. That was ok with me as I was enjoying the moon and the shadows it threw across the mountains. The miles rolled by quickly as we passed through small towns with Colorado sounding names like Rifle and Eagle. Soon we were approaching Glenwood Springs, which boasted the world's largest hot springs swimming pool. Glenwood Springs received a lot of promotion as a destination place for vacationers but the magnificent canyon that we had to drive through before getting into the town was completely ignored. With canyon walls going straight up and the beautiful Colorado River flowing through it, the canyon was awe-inspiring. The river was flowing heavily and Mr. Moore mentioned that it was due to the early run off of the snow pack. I was somewhat surprised to see that the stream was not wide at all in some places. When I rolled the car window down I could hear the roar of the water as it echoed off the canyon walls on its trip to the Grand Canyon. At that moment I didn't think I had ever seen anything more beautiful. I thought of the men who had over a century ago trekked over these enormous peaks, never knowing what was on the other side. I wondered what they would think of their mountains now. Somehow I felt they would be disappointed in what we call progress. However, I suppose that is the reason they were willing to endure the hardships they suffered during the time they spent finding new trails to the west coast. Perhaps they would be happy with the results. At that particular moment I was grateful for their adventurous spirit.

Once we were out of Glenwood Springs, the terrain changed from high peaks to a more level landscape with steep mesas and tabletop mountains. I knew we had come to the western slope of Colorado. Here Mr. Moore could make up time lost in the mountains. He kept the speed at a constant sixty-five and we stopped only briefly in Grand Junction for him to pick up coffee for his thermos. Less than an hour later we crossed the Utah border and I knew soon we would be in Salt Lake City, where I planned to spend the day and night.

We arrived in the Mormon capitol just as the sun was beginning to rise over the mountains that surround Salt Lake. It is a beautiful city surrounded by the Wasatch Mountains and the thing I noticed immediately was how clean it appeared to be. Salt Lake has enormously wide streets and boulevards. I remember reading that when the Mormons laid out the city they specified that the streets should be wide enough for two teams of oxen with wagons to make a complete turn. Too bad other cities had not had the same foresight as the Mormons.

Salt Lake was home for Mr. Moore so he let me out in the middle of downtown, telling me there were a number of hotels I could choose from. We shook hands and he left me with a final piece of advice: "Remember," he said, "any job worth having is worth doing right." It sounded like something my father would say. I had the impression that Mr. Moore didn't have much confidence in the younger generation, particularly their work habits.

I planned to visit the Mormon Temple and take the tour because I was interested in their history and their unique beliefs. I didn't believe in Mormonism or much of anything else. I just wanted to see what it was that old John Smith and Brigham Young had done that inspired or motivated people to build such monuments. Even though I didn't believe in their version of the Bible and certainly not the story of the angel Moroni receiving the true word of God, I still had to admire them for their perseverance. I remembered enough of my history to know that the Mormons were one of the most persecuted minorities in our nation's history. I knew they had been run out of New York, Illinois and Missouri before finally settling in Utah. I could only guess that this beautiful but desolate location must have seemed like a place where they could practice their religion without ever again having to worry about what other people thought.

After riding across the Rockies, I was ready for a bed. I walked around for a while to work out the kinks and then checked into the Hotel Utah. The place was old, but immaculate. The clerk behind the desk treated me just like I was a businessman in a three-piece suit and motioned for one of the bellhops to get my luggage. I only had the one piece, and said I would take it up myself. The bellhop didn't seem to mind. He probably didn't think I was good for much of a tip anyway.

I sat my bag in the closet and stretched out on the bed, not even bothering to get undressed. I awoke at seven and, after another ten minutes in the shower, I decided it was time to eat and maybe check out what the nightlife was like. If the town was as liberal as Brigham Young, I was ready for a good evening. Unfortunately I soon discovered that Brigham Young may have had some liberal views on marriage, but he was certainly conservative on other matters.

The hotel restaurant was my first stop and, unfortunately, it was a mistake. I ordered a sirloin strip with baked potato and salad. The steak was small and cold, the potato overcooked, and the salad was warm as if it had been sitting out all day. The roll that accompanied the meal was apparently baked to be eaten with a knife and fork. A giant, round mass of cooked dough that was larger than the plate it sat on defied me to break it open. I called the waitress back and told her the roll was old.

"Can't be," she said defiantly, "baked them this morning."

"I don't care when it was baked, its tough and old," I persisted.

"It's supposed to be tough," the waitress countered, looking at me like I was a fool for not understanding this most basic rule of bread baking. I knew I wasn't going to win this argument.

"Look," I said, "do you have any plain bread, white, wheat, anything else besides this roll?"

"Yeah, I suppose we do," she answered, a bit grudgingly I thought.

"Good, would you bring me a couple of slices please?"

"Ok," she said doubtfully, "but that roll was baked just this morning."

By the time she returned I had managed to finish half the steak and potato before giving up. I left the two pieces of Wonder Bread she had brought me on the plate. They were old and dry.

I paid my check, leaving the waitress a small tip, and walked out into the cool night air. Nightlife in Salt Lake definitely seemed to be suffering from the Mormon influence. Few bars and clubs were open and I had walked about three blocks before I found one that looked inviting enough to go inside. I found a small table and ordered bourbon on the rocks with water on the side. The waitress indicated that I would have to go to the state liquor store adjacent to the club and pick up my bourbon. Utah, it seemed, didn't believe in mixing the business of selling alcohol with the pleasure of drinking it in the same building. Apparently old Brigham Young declared alcohol and caffeine off limits to all good Mormons. I suppose that explained the popularity of orange drinks sold everywhere. However, as I would soon discover, a lot of the good Mormons were known to sneak a few beers or a cup of coffee now and then. These Mormons were referred to as "Jack Mormons," for reasons I was never able to understand.

I didn't understand the waitress so she patiently explained that the club could not sell liquor, only the state. I could tell that she was used to explaining this unique law to tourists and thirsty travelers. I walked out of the club and into the state-owned liquor store next door, where the shelves were filled with small bottles of liquor, just large enough for one drink. I ordered two bottles of Jack Daniels and the clerk asked for six dollars. I figured the state must have been doing pretty good in the liquor business. I took the bottles back into the bar and asked the waitress for a glass of water and some ice. When she brought it she asked for a dollar fifty. *Not bad for water*, I thought to myself. I finished the whiskey, left another small tip, and walked back to my hotel and went straight to bed.

I awoke the next morning at eight o'clock and after taking a long shower gathered my shaving kit and one piece of luggage and checked out of the hotel. I walked out into bright sunshine with puffy white clouds tinged with blue dotting the sky. It looked like it would be a good day for hitchhiking. I skipped the hotel coffee shop and found a cafe a couple of blocks away where I had a breakfast of blueberry waffles and coffee. I noticed I was one of the few with a coffee cup in front of me. I paid my check and headed toward Mormon Square for my tour. Even though I was anxious to get on the road again I knew I would regret not seeing the Temple and the history of the Mormons from their perspective.

I joined up with about fifteen other people for a tour of the facility but once we got underway I broke off from the group to conduct my own tour. Standing in the mammoth structure I could almost feel Brigham Young's presence. I wondered if he would approve of the changes in his church, especially since the Mormons had to give up the practice of polygamy in order to gain statehood. It seemed to me that he had a good deal going for himself. As I remembered, he had nineteen wives. I didn't see how you could argue with anyone who gets so many people to agree that he is entitled to the pick of all the young women just for the asking. I imagined that he would make one hell of a salesman.

I spent about an hour and a half walking around and reading about the history and religious beliefs of the Mormons, which was fascinating, but not enough to make me want to join them. When I glanced at my watch I saw it was approaching twelve o'clock and decided it was time to hit the road. I caught a cab right outside the Temple and had the driver take me to the edge of town. Getting a ride from downtown was impossible.

I paid the cabby three bucks and got out. Since it was a nice day, I picked up my bag and started walking. I don't know how many miles I walked. I was too intent on the scenery to care. As I walked, I noticed the mountains more than anything else. It looked as if someone had taken a giant crayon and marked a ring around the top of them. I recalled a geology professor saying something about the water level reaching near the top of mountains in North America, hundreds of thousands of years ago. When the professor spoke about it I wasn't too impressed, but now actually seeing what it was that he was talking about made quite a different impression on me. I tried to imagine what the area must have looked like covered with all that water. I knew the mountains were several thousand feet high so it was difficult to visualize such a vast expanse of ocean.

Eventually, a farmer in a pickup truck picked me up and we rode to Tremonton, Utah, whose claim to fame if I believed the billboard at the edge of town, was that it was the home of Al Orerter, Olympic champion in the discus throw. I thought Tremonton was lucky to have something for a claim to fame, because it was not going to be on my list of top ten places to visit again.

I had not been in Tremonton long before a late model green Plymouth stopped. The driver was named Otto and in the years since, I have found few people that I remember as fondly and as well as Otto and his family.

He was a giant of a man with huge arms and shoulders. But, his thumbs were unique. They were enormously thick, with long black hair sprouting everywhere and nails that looked like polished ivory. I knew that if ever there were a thumb wrestling championship, Otto would undoubtedly win.

He was a sugar beet farmer who lived in Pocatello, Idaho. His son, James, had just graduated from Brigham Young University the night before and he was driving back home now, after attending the ceremony. James was also somewhere on the highway, headed back to Pocatello to the farm where he was going to become a partner in the family farming operations. I could tell by the way Otto talked about the farm, James, and his family, that this was a day he had dreamed about and worked toward for a long time. It was reassuring to know that such family loyalty and love existed. James had chosen Brigham Young for the business school and it was evident Otto intended to let him be the business manager of the farm.

Otto kept me informed about the country, particularly the Mormons whom he seemed to know a great deal about, despite the fact that he was a Lutheran. He was quick to point out that being a Lutheran placed him in a decided minority, as seventy per cent of the population in the area was Mormon. He seemed unusually proud that James had attended Brigham Young University. Even though I didn't know much about the school I knew it was somewhat unusual to have anyone but Mormons attending.

Otto knew a lot about the history of Utah, the Mormons and the whole area. While I enjoyed his stories, I wasn't convinced about all of them.

Once, as we neared Pocatello, he took a side road that was apparently a shortcut. As we passed the farms, he began to mention the names of people who owned them and usually some short story about the family background. I was astonished that he could actually know that much about the people since we were apparently still quite a ways from his own home.

We passed one field where an old man was just getting off a huge John Deere tractor near the fencerow. Otto waved to him as the old man was waving back. Otto pulled the car to the side of the road, killed the engine and got out.

"I'll just be a minute," he said.

As he talked to the man in the field, I noticed that about a hundred yards away was a neat white frame farmhouse. Then, I noticed that about another hundred yards to the north sat an identical house. It appeared to be slightly more weathered and in need of a new coat of paint. After about ten minutes, of animated conversation with the old man, Otto came back and we left.

"That was Bud McGuire," he said. "Good farmer. Says he's going to make a lot of potatoes this year."

"Good," I replied, since I couldn't think of anything else to say. My knowledge of potatoes was limited to fried, mashed and baked.

"He's a Mormon," Otto went on. "See those two houses?" He indicated the two I had been looking at. "Everyone knows Mormons can't practice polygamy," he said. "But how do you tell somebody to change their religion? Well, old Bud there had two wives for a while. He built those two houses identical to each other for each wife. Sadie, the oldest wife, died about ten years ago. I never really knew his other wife. Seems she died just a year or two after they were married. Anyway, that's what people say. Lots of older Mormons kept right on taking wives after the government passed the law against polygamy. Nowadays, they're just like everyone else. One woman ought to be enough for any man as I see it. Providing, of course, she's the right woman," he chuckled.

I asked him how they avoided trouble with the law if they couldn't have more than one wife.

"Oh, they don't record the marriage with the state or county, they just have a religious ceremony," he explained. "That way the state can't prove that the law has been broken. There's still a few practicing polygamists around, but not very many. Why just the other day I read about a man down in Brigham City that had quadruplets by one wife and he already had seven children by her sister. They kind of like to keep everything in the family, if you know what I mean," he explained with a wink. "I can't imagine a man wanting to marry his sister-in-law. Lord knows I don't want anything to do with mine. Betty can be meaner than a rattlesnake in heat," he said more to himself than to me.

He kept telling stories about the Mormons and Utah until we reached his farm. It was a beautiful farm, like the ones you see advertised in farm magazines. Fat Holstein cattle grazed in lush green pastures, a big white barn with a red brick silo stood behind a wooden rail fence. I could see why he was a happy man. He insisted that I meet his family.

The family consisted of Otto's wife, grandmother, grandfather, and a young daughter about sixteen. Introductions were made all around with Trisha, the daughter, blushing noticeably when I took her hand to shake it. She was a pretty girl, tall and thin with long auburn hair tied back in a ponytail. They were all busy in the kitchen preparing a welcome home dinner for the new college graduate. Otto showed me the bath, in case I wanted to wash up before dinner. He had never asked me if I wanted to eat, he just apparently took it for granted that I would.

James, the new college graduate, soon arrived to much backslapping and hugs and congratulations from all the family. I wanted to ask why Otto was the only one in the family to attend the graduation, but figured it was none of my business. Clearly, he was a man in charge of his family and I didn't want to offend anyone. James and I shook hands and I offered my congratulations to those of his family on his graduation.

If all farmers ate the way Otto's family did, then I know I missed something by not living on a real farm. The family clearly loved and respected Otto. No one sat down until he came to the table.

The meal featured fried chicken that was golden and crispy on the outside but juicy and tender on the inside. A large platter of fried steak, plus potatoes, gravy, corn, squash, green beans, home-baked bread and two kinds of pies completed the meal.

During the meal they all politely asked questions, mainly about Oklahoma and farmland. I'm afraid I wasn't much help there, however. Only Otto had been as far south as Texas and he talked knowledgeably about the good farmland. His daughter kept stealing glances at me throughout the meal and once when we made eye contact she quickly excused herself to get more iced tea. I couldn't help but compare her future with that of James. I guessed that she would probably marry a local farm boy and settle into the lifestyle of her mother and grandmother, who seemed to be perfectly happy with theirs. Still, when she discovered that I was hitchhiking all the way to Washington she was full of questions until her mother gave her a disapproving look. It was not polite to ask too many questions.

After the meal, I said my good-byes and thanks for the dinner. James and I left for Boise. He was going there to make arrangements for a new tractor to be delivered to the farm. It was his first major assignment as the new partner and it signified that he was truly a full member in the family business.

The trip to Boise was uneventful and I managed to catch a little sleep. James was obviously preoccupied with his thoughts about his new role in the farm and said little. He dropped me off at the Boise

Hotel in downtown and headed for the John Deere dealer or to find a hotel of his own since he would be staying the night. I enjoyed watching his excitement about his new position in the family business. I couldn't help but wonder where I would be in a couple of years and if my life would be in similar order. James was only a couple of years older than me and it seemed like he had his whole life planned. Still, I wondered just how much of the planning he had done for himself and if he would ever regret moving back to the family farm. I hoped not.

The Boise Hotel was probably a showpiece in its day, but unfortunately its day had come and gone. Like so many of the grand old hotels, it had fallen victim to the endless array of Holiday Inns and other chains that lined outskirts of any city of over thirty thousand people.

I love old hotels and this one was a great one with halls large enough for four people to walk down them shoulder to shoulder. It had a huge winding staircase with the wooden banisters polished smooth from the thousands of hands that had moved up and down them. The carpet was threadbare, but spotless, and I wondered how many more cleaning it could take before the wood floor would begin to show through. The ceilings were stamped tin and closer inspection revealed that all the parts together displayed a mosaic image of mountains, streams and wildlife common to Idaho. The walls were covered with beautiful old pictures of more mountains, Indians and trappers. The next day I learned that the hotel was scheduled for demolition to make way for a new, modern grand hotel with covered parking. *More progress*, I thought.

I was so tired from the trip I sacked out on the lumpy old bed, intending to rest for just a few minutes, but when I awoke it was already nine o'clock. I showered, shaved and felt like eating again, although I certainly shouldn't have been hungry after the meal at Otto's.

I decided against the hotel coffee shop after recalling my meal at the Hotel Utah. I also wanted to see if the nightlife in Boise was any different than in Utah. I quickly discovered that there wasn't much difference between the two cities and I questioned whether or not that was due to the Mormon influence. After walking a couple of blocks I decided on a pizzeria that seemed to be popular with the local teenagers. I found a small booth at the back and ordered a pepperoni with mushrooms and a beer. The waitress, who was about eighteen, brought my beer in a tall frosty mug that had little slivers of ice running down the side. You could forget those beer makers who suggested that their brew be drunk at forty-five degrees. I finished the beer in three long drinks and ordered another. The pizza tasted good, and had lots of extra cheese. It went well with the cold beer and the music the teenagers were playing on a beautiful old Wurlitzer jukebox. I suddenly felt old and tired as I listened to the music and watched the group of kids horsing around the jukebox. *That was a hell of a note,* I thought. Twenty-one and feeling old. I paid my tab and left.

    I decided on the hotel coffee shop for breakfast the next morning since it seemed to be a busy and popular place. I picked up the Boise paper at the counter. There wasn't much happening in Boise or anywhere else in the country it seemed. The Boise Braves were on a losing streak, seven in a row. Management was crying the parent club was taking all the talent. Locally, a county commissioner was under investigation for alleged misuse of county funds. The world it seemed was the same, be it Boise or Boston.

    I caught a cab to the edge of Boise and waited for a ride. After about five minutes a young guy in another Volkswagen stopped. He was going to Ontario, Oregon, and that was good enough for me. The scenery was beautiful and I settled back in the small seat just to enjoy. The driver was about twenty-five and he didn't talk much. That was all right with me, since I didn't feel like talking. I had no idea how far it was to Ontario but about an hour and a half later just as we crossed the Idaho line into Oregon the driver announced we were there. He pulled the Volkswagen off on the side of the road and let me out on what appeared to be a main highway. I hadn't been standing there more than ten minutes when it began to drizzle, then sprinkle. Huge dark clouds were rolling in over the mountains and I could see flashes of lightning that looked like someone turning lights on and off quickly in a dark room. The ominous sound of rolling thunder cascaded off the near by mountains with each clap getting louder. I searched both sides of the highway for a gas station or some place I could take cover if the storm got too bad. There was nothing in sight. I was afraid I might be stuck there for quite a while. I thought about walking, but the place I had was near an off ramp and I knew that was probably the best location to catch a ride. The rain was getting harder and I had been standing there for almost half an hour, when a big, yellow Hertz rent-a-truck came tearing by and then I saw the brake lights flash. I grabbed my bag and ran the guy down before he had a chance to change his mind. The driver extended his hand and introduced himself as Max.

"Mark," I said, shaking his hand, "and I'm really glad to meet you."

Max was about forty years old, I guessed, with the kind of lean wiry build that I was used to seeing on bull riders. He sported a pencil thin mustache and a small ragged goatee. He wore a black tee shirt with cigarettes rolled up into the sleeve. On anyone else it would have been just a laughable affectation, but it suited Max perfectly. He had a gold front tooth that flashed when he smiled. He reminded me of a guy who used to work at the ice plant in my hometown. Back then, before the beginning of Seven-Elevens and ice machines, small towns in Oklahoma had an ice plant to supply restaurants and businesses. There were even some homes in the town that still had ice delivered and stored in old wooden iceboxes. I remembered that as kids we would follow the delivery truck during the summer grabbing pieces of the ice chips from the back of the truck. They were as refreshing to us as any cold drink could have been. Even though I hadn't thought about it in years, I recalled the driver of the ice truck was named Mutt. Max reminded me a lot of him.

He handed me a rag, the kind service stations use to clean windshields. I used it to mop at the water on my face and hair. The rain was coming down in huge droplets that smacked the windshield hard and I wondered if some of it wasn't mixed with hail. Even though it was June, the air was chilly at this altitude. The thin sport shirt I was wearing clung to me and I could feel water running down the small of my back. Max obligingly turned on the heater in the truck to help me dry faster.

Since I had been waiting on a ride for at least half an hour, I was curious why anyone in a rent-a-truck would stop in a downpour for a hitchhiker. I posed the question to Max.

"Simple," he replied, "I was getting sleepy and I have to make it to Pendleton by three o'clock to deliver this load of furniture. I need someone to talk to so I won't fall asleep at the wheel."

I had no intention of letting him fall asleep, not on those mountain roads. It seemed like all I had seen since Denver was the top of a mountain road. I was ready for the flatlands already, but the drivers in this part of the country didn't seem to notice the sheer drop-offs, guarded sometimes by only a narrow rail, which couldn't have stopped a bicycle. I could imagine Max taking us over the edge of a ten-thousand-foot mountain with both of us asleep. I thought about my mother and how she would never forgive me if that happened. She was the champion worrywart and warned me repeatedly about the dangers of hitchhiking when I told her I was going to Washington for the summer. At that moment I almost wished I had taken her advice and stayed home for the summer.

The cab was getting warm and making me drowsy, so I asked Max to turn the heater off. He did. If it was talk he needed, then I was prepared. We talked about everything: the weather, Oklahoma, Oregon, his job, my job, women, liquor, politics, religion and a lot of other things which I'm sure neither of us knew anything about. Like most strangers who first meet, we could lie as much as we wanted since we knew we would never see each other again. When I thought about it maybe those kinds of lies are really the truest form of honesty. People just being themselves knowing they don't have to answer to anyone and haven't caused any harm.

The scenery between Ontario and Pendleton was some of the most spectacular I had seen on my trip. High mountains on all sides, highways that seemed to climb straight up the mountains and then long downgrades with a view for miles. Often, at the top, I could see small lakes, their water as blue as sapphires, nestled in distance mountain meadows. Snow glistened at the top and on some parts of the road where it had mounded into deep drifts. A road sign welcomed us to Baker, Oregon, and proclaimed it to be the county seat of Baker County. I had never seen a more beautiful yet rugged location in my life. Max told me that the towering mountain that dominated the view as we drove into town was called the Matterhorn. I never knew if that was the real name or one that the locals had given it. Wispy white and blue clouds teased the top of the mountain occasionally giving me a glimpse of its jagged snow capped peak. Max pulled into a local truck stop and announced that he had to have a "cup of java" to keep him going for the rest of the trip. The coffee was good and so was the coconut cream pie I bought for us. I still had fifty bucks and I knew I would be in Washington before nightfall, so I was feeling benevolent.

The scenery just kept getting more spectacular and the mountains higher until, finally, we reached the top of a mountain and the sign said: "Downgrade next seven miles." Max really made good time on downgrades. He opened up the truck so that it sounded like a jet about to take off. He told me how the trucking companies put governors on their vehicles to keep drivers from really tearing them up. However, governors didn't help that much when he was on a downgrade, so Max let her rip down those mountainsides and I kept looking at those narrow roads and long drops. I was thinking about my mother again and her usual doomsday attitude that something terrible would happen to me. I sure hoped Max wasn't going to prove her right.

He had a habit of looking at me while talking and this, of course, meant he couldn't look at the road. This made me nervous. I really didn't seem to have much of a choice. I could either let Max go to sleep on a mountain road and run off the side or talk to him and hope that he stayed awake long enough for us to get to Pendleton.

I breathed easier after we reached the bottom and the road seemed to be a little straighter for a while. At least we seemed to be in hill country and not mountains, so Max and I got the conversation going again. It was at this point he brought up the subject of guns. I don't know how it came up, but he told me to look in the glove box of the truck. I opened it and there lay two, big, ugly pistols. For a minute I thought crazily, *What if this guy is a nut who goes around picking up hitchhikers and then shoots and robs them.* More thoughts of my mother and her prophecy ran through my head. Then I realized he probably wouldn't be showing me the guns if that were what he had in mind. For that matter, I could just as easily have robbed him. Really, when I thought about it, I decided Max wasn't too smart to be showing me the guns at all. Hell, for all he knew, I could be a kook who could kill him, steal his truck and the load of furniture. I said what I hoped was the proper thing about the guns and gingerly placed them back in the glove box. For some reason, guns were never high on my list of favorite things. I've never owned one and never really wanted one.

Max was really proud of those two pistols though, so I felt obliged to try and talk a little about how nice they were. But what do you say nice about a gun? "Wow, bet this would blow somebody's brains out," or, "Shit, bet this baby could knock a hole in someone." Somehow that just didn't seem like the right thing, so I tried to change the subject.

Max was making good time despite the load, the roads, and the governor and in about an hour we reached Pendleton. All I could think of was the Pendleton Rodeo, one of the more famous ones on the rodeo circuit. I would have given a lot to have seen it and maybe someday will. It brought back memories of the summer following my high school graduation when on a dare I entered the bull-riding event at a small town rodeo. The fact that I had consumed several bottles of beer when I accepted the challenge probably had a lot to do with making such a foolish decision.

As things turned out I won some money and ended up riding all summer to make enough to pay for my college tuition the next year. It was the fastest way to make money that I could think of but not the smartest. Staying astride eighteen hundred pounds of angry bull for eight seconds is not the easiest or safest job in the world. Anyway, I gave it up after seeing a rider killed after getting kicked in the head. I still remember the sound it made, like a large watermelon being dropped onto pavement. Still, I would rather ride a bull than a horse because a bull is at least predictable. They are always in a bad mood. The thing about a bull is that it will throw its head back towards you while you are coming forward and smash you in the mouth with his horns or head. Catching a mouthful of horns and bone from an irritated bull has ended the career of many a cowboy. Riders who survive for any length of time are generally missing their front teeth. I wanted to keep all of mine so I quit after two seasons. Nevertheless, I would have loved to see Penelton, since it featured the best riders and bulls on the circuit.

Max pulled the big truck over to the side of the road and I gathered my luggage and hopped out. We shook hands while I thanked him for the ride as he roared off in a cloud of black smoke. I knew with any luck, I would be in Strasborg in a short while and I was getting anxious to be there. I threw my bag down on the road and sat down on it, admiring the view. The terrain had changed in the last couple of hours from towering mountain peaks to rolling hills. They were covered in lush green vegetation that I recognized as wheat. It would not be ready for harvest until much later in the summer and into September. I knew that this was a fertile area that ran from Pendleton on past Strasborg and back into the Yakima Valley. While some wheat was grown in the area the real crops were fruit, mainly apples, barley, which went into the making of beer and of course the most famous crop and the reason for my being there: peas. If the literature that the company had sent me was correct, virtually all of the green peas consumed in the United States were grown within a few miles of where I was sitting. I guess I was supposed to be impressed but I found it amusing that anyone would want to be known as the pea capitol of the world.

About twenty minutes later a blue and white, dust covered '53 Chevy pulled up beside me and an old man with a full beard sitting on the passenger side, asked if I want a ride.

"You bet," I said, "if you're going towards Strasborg."

"Going to Milton-Freewater," Whiskers answered, "but you're welcome to come along."

The driver was about the same age as Whiskers, which I guess to be somewhere near seventy, although it was hard to tell. Unlike his passenger, the driver didn't quite have a full beard, more like he hadn't shaved in a week.

"Name's Ben," Whiskers said, barely turning in his seat. "This here's Tip," he motioned toward the driver who grunted a greeting. He reached under the seat and pulled out a Hamms beer, which he opened and handed to me. It was good, still cold. I had never tried Hamms.

"So you're going to pick peas?" Ben questioned.

"How did you know that?" I asked, curious, since I hadn't said anything about being on my way to work in the pea harvest.

"What else can a young buck do in Strasborg but pick peas?" He laughed. "Besides, you all have been coming through here all week now."

"Who has?" I asked.

"Young bucks like yourself," Ben snorted. "Who else wants to go to Strasborg? Hot as hell, dusty too. Hours are long every damn day. Why did you come up here, boy? Where you from anyway?" he asked me all at once.

"Oklahoma," I answered.

"Oklahoma," Ben snorted again, "now why the hell didn't you stay there and work? They got lots of pretty women in Oklahoma, as I remember."

"I couldn't find a job there. Besides, I wanted to see the country," I told him a little defensively.

"Ain't nothing to see," Ben answered in somber tones. "Just dirt and ugly women."

"Bet you didn't know," he went on, "Strasborg has more ugly women than any town in Washington? Hell, maybe the United States, or the whole damn world. Yep, more than the whole damn world," he said sadly, really more to himself than to me, I thought.

Strasborg didn't seem too promising. I was beginning to worry about my summer in Washington.

"It's the peas," Ben said, drawing on his beer.

"What?" I asked, not understanding what he was talking about.

"The peas," Ben replied, "the peas, that's what makes Strasborg women so God-awful ugly. They just sit around and eat peas like they were peanuts, so that they get all fat and ugly." He gave a little shudder to his shoulders as if the very thought of it made him ill. "Just you wait, boy. You'll see." He laughed and slapped his knee, spilling a little of his beer.

Tip hadn't said a word the whole time and I was wondering if maybe he was drunk and asleep at the wheel, but he kept the old Chevy on a steady course.

"Where you staying tonight?" Ben asked suddenly.

"Strasborg, I guess, if I get there."

"Could stay at our house," Ben offered, "but we loaned it to some drunks this afternoon."

I didn't ask why he was loaning his house to drunks, because I was sure it would take a longer explanation than I cared to hear.

The '53 Chevy rolled along, me drinking beer, Tip just driving, not talking, and Ben carrying on a conversation with the two of us, and sometimes himself.

"Tell you what," Ben announced, as if he had just come up with the answer to a pressing world problem. "You just go into Walla Walla. Or better yet, Spokane, if you get a chance. Now there's where the real women are. Young buck like you shouldn't have any problem at all in finding a woman."

"I know all about the cannery." Ben started off in a new vein now that he had the woman situation solved.

"You watch they don't dock you the last fifteen minutes every day," he warned me. "Fifteen minutes don't sound like much, but you add it up, it's almost two hours a week. Take that times three hundred workers, see what you got. Thousands of dollars a year not being paid in wages, that's what you got," he roared and slapped the dash of the old Chevy, causing the dust to fly all the way to the back seat where I was finishing another beer.

"Something else," Ben continued. "Don't eat at the commissary any more than you have to. Bastard Bert charges an arm and a leg for beans. No sir, you go into town to eat. Go to the Palm Club. They'll give you a decent hamburger anyway, real beef, not that horsemeat Bert serves. And stay away from them whoring daughters of his, unless you want the crabs." He rattled on, intent on saving me from upset stomachs and venereal disease.

I didn't know why Ben was dispensing all the free advice, since I had just met him, but I was trying to make a mental note of all he said. It was an almost impossible task since he kept changing topics with almost every breath. Anyway, I figured someone who would loan his house to a bunch of drunks probably had been around enough to know what he was talking about.

"Something else," he started again, turning around in the seat to face me. "You tell that bastard, Joe, I said to give you a corner bunk and extra blankets or I'll be up to kick his ass. You got that?" he asked. "Corner bunk and extra blankets."

"I got it," I said, "but who is Joe?"

"Joe, Joe Bunkhouse, anyway that's all I've ever known him by," said Ben. "You won't know him by anything else either," he continued. "Just tell him you know me and I'll be up to see him in a couple of weeks and I'll expect to see you in a corner bunk with extra blankets. He stays drunk all the time anyway," Ben said. "Sleeps all day and stays drunk all night. He can be mean when he's drunk, so stay out of his way," Ben warned in an ominous tone. "Other than that, he ain't a bad old fart."

With that announcement, we reached a city limits sign that said Milton-Freewater, Green River Ordinance in effect. I would be parting company with Ben and Tip, so Tip pulled the old Chevy over to the side of the road and we drank the last two Hamms, sort of as a good-bye drink. I never saw either one of them again and, to this day, I wonder if they got their house back from the drunks they loaned it to. I also never knew if Tip could talk.

Milton-Freewater was just a small town with quiet streets. It was not unlike the one I had grown up in Oklahoma. For a minute I was homesick and really questioned if I was making a mistake in coming all this distance for a job that didn't sound too promising if I believed everything that Ben had told me.

I had been waiting at the edge of town for ten minutes or so, when a green Ford came by. I could see the driver was a kid and it looked like a woman and a young guy also in the front seat. The driver slammed on his brakes and the gravel flew over me and my bag as he skidded to a stop. I wasn't sure I wanted to ride with this guy. *Hell, I thought, I've only got thirty miles or so and I may not get another ride.* So I grabbed my bag and took off. The Ford was backing up and weaving uncertainly.

The driver was about eighteen and I knew right off he was a smart ass. The other guy looked to be a couple of years older. The woman must have been pushing forty. She was wearing jeans and a halter-top that was way too small for what it was holding. All three of them were drinking Hamms beer.

Smart Ass said, "Going to Strasborg to pick peas, ain't cha?"

"Yeah," I said, not sure it was any of his business.

"Your're going to hate it," he replied.

"How do you know?" I asked him.

"Work your ass off all day and get it kicked every time you come into town," he sneered at me through the rear view mirror.

"What do you mean by that?" I wanted to know, although I was pretty sure what he had in mind.

"Every time you come into town, we kick your ass," he replied as if that was the most obvious thing in the world to know. "We don't like all you college boys thinking you're top shit, so we just whip your butt every chance we get," he continued, obviously enjoying the thought.

"If that's so, then why did you pick me up?" I asked.

He eyed me in the rear view mirror. "You getting smart with me college boy?" he wanted to know through speech slurred by too many beers.

It was easy to see that this guy had a serious problem with anyone he thought to be an outsider. Like a lot of people I have known he had a prejudice against anyone that was smarter than themselves. I could see that included just about everyone with an IQ over seventy as far as he was concerned.

"Come on, Johnny," the older guy said, "Knock it off. You talk too much."

"Talk all I want to," Johnny shot back, spewing beer over the woman.

"Yeah, yeah," the older guy said wearily. "Here," he turned in the seat and tossed me a Hamms. "Have a beer and don't mind Johnny. He runs off at the mouth too much."

"What you doing, giving my beer away," Smart Ass challenged.

"It ain't your beer," the other guy said, "I paid for it and I'm giving one to my friend." I knew the guy was only being friendly to irritate Johnny but I wasn't sure I wanted him any madder than he already seemed to be, especially since he was driving.

The woman touched Johnny's shoulder and said, "Come on, Johnny, be nice now. You're spoiling the party by being that way."

"Sure," he growled, still eyeing me in the rear view mirror. "I'll be nice 'til we get to Strasborg."

I recognized a threat when I heard one and I was sure Johnny wasn't going to keep his promise to be nice.

It was only a few miles from Milton-Freewater to Strasborg, but we had to stop every five miles, it seemed, for Johnny to take a piss. He paid no attention to the passing cars as he would just go to the side of the road, unzip his pants and take care of business. Each time, he would point at me and repeat, "Just wait, college boy. Your time is coming." I had an uneasy feeling that my arrival in Strasborg was not going to be a pleasant ending to my trip.

The old Ford coughed the last two miles into Strasborg and I wasn't sure if either one of us was going to make it to the headquarters of the plant. We arrived in Strasborg and I could see why Ben had described it in such depressing terms. I could see the entire business district from one end of town to the other. Small, single story structures lined both sides of the main street. A hot, dry wind was blowing someone's trash down the dirty and dilapidated sidewalks. A single cur dog with its ribs showing prominently poked his nose into each empty sack hoping for someone's discarded lunch. *Welcome to Strasborg,* I thought.

We drove to the end of town, turned down a narrow street, crossed a bridge and headed up a dusty unpaved road that led to the plant and living quarters.

The bunkhouse was just that. A large, dirty, white building with cracks big enough to stick a finger through sat at the end of the road. Train tracks ran only twenty-five feet from the back of it.

The Ford began to sputter, leap and then, with a shudder, came to a halt. I waited for the inevitable conflict with Johnny who by now was totally drunk and in an even meaner mood than when he picked me up.

"Son of a bitch," Johnny fumed as he kicked the door open. I thought for a moment he was talking to me.

"What's wrong, honey?" the woman asked, stroking Johnny's arm.

"How the hell am I supposed to know?" he yelled, kicking a tire.

The other guy popped a Hamms and smiled. "Look at your gas gauge, dumb ass," he said to Johnny. "You ain't got no gas."

Johnny was livid. I took the opportunity to start walking toward the bunkhouse. I couldn't help but laugh as I thought about the irony of it all while I set my bag on the steps of the bunkhouse and watched Johnny start walking toward town for gasoline. The woman and the other guy were enjoying another beer.

I walked into the nearly deserted bunkhouse. It was well over a hundred and fifty feet long, with single, army-type cots spaced about three feet apart. It smelled of dust and the accumulation of years of cigarette smoke and stale beer. Between each bed was a single locker with a lock on it. At one end were the communal showers with lavatories to serve the whole bunkhouse. In one corner, by itself, was a bed with a double locker and a footlocker underneath the bed. Next to it was obviously the storeroom with a window in it, where I could see mattresses and blankets piled on the shelves and floor.

That, I thought, *must be Joe's bunk*. Almost at that instant, an old man with a week's growth of bead and the largest beer gut I have ever seen, came around the corner of the storeroom. He was holding a pint of Jim Beam in his hand and had a cold cigar stub in his mouth.

"Hello," I ventured.

His response was to totally ignore me. Going to the footlocker, he took a heavy key ring from his pocket and, unlocking the chest, deposited the Jim Beam.

I tried again. "I guess I'm supposed to check in with you," I said.

He took the cigar stub out of his mouth and eyed me carefully. "If you're aiming to work her, you check in with me," he said.

Encouraged by his response I said, "Ben told me to ask for a corner bunk and extra blankets."

"Look sonny," he eyed me with bloodshot watery eyes, "I don't know no Ben and you take what I give you, understand? You don't give me no shit, keep quiet when you're supposed to and we'll get along just fine. Get out of line and I'll kick our ass so hard and fast you'll think your flying. Understand?"

I nodded, thinking that the people in Strasborg sure enjoyed kicking ass a hell of a lot.

"Okay," he said, "what's your name?"

"James" I answered.

He went to the storeroom coming back with a clipboard and flipping some pages, scanned the list of names until, finding mine, he checked it off.

"Come on," he ordered me.

I didn't get my corner bunk. I got two blankets, two sheets and a pillowcase. Bunkhouse Joe, or whatever the hell his name was, kept muttering all the time about college boys, Okies and the lousy weather.

"We go in order, see," Joe said. "You can have any bunk after those first two by that wall, thems already taken. You're responsible for your own laundry, we don't run no maid service around here" he advised me with a stare that was as cold and dead as his cigar.

The bunks were made and a footlocker sat at the end of each. They didn't look occupied, but I wasn't going to argue with beer belly, so I took my bag to the third cot and dumped everything on top of it.

"You got a lock?" Bunkhouse asked.

"Yeah, a combination."

"Good," Joe said, "Use it, the ones here don't work and the dirty bastards steal you blind, but don't come crying to me if it happens. I can't do nothing about it, understand?"

"Sure," I said, "You don't have to worry about me. I can take care of myself."

"Good, see that you do" he muttered, as he shuffled off towards his Jim Beam.

I made my bunk, stored my clothes and realized I was suddenly hungry. It was seven o'clock and I hadn't eaten since the pie and coffee with Max. The beer I had been drinking had apparently kept my appetite in check. *If everyone up here drinks this much*, I thought, *I can see myself going home absolutely skinny and having to face Mother, who always worries that I don't eat enough.*

After taking a shower and cleaning up my clothes as best I could, I decided to walk into town and check out the Palm Club that Ben had mentioned. A hamburger sounded really good now.

I walked the quarter mile back into town, taking time to admire the view. I noticed the Ford with Johnny and the other two people was gone and felt relief.

The bunkhouse sat in the bottom of a valley, with small mountains surrounding it. It looked very much like the picture on a can of peas. Any minute, I expected to see a giant rise from the behind the hills and begin walking with me.

The Palm Club was one of those comfortable cafe bars that enjoys a local reputation and can survive just from business it gets from the townspeople. The fact that it was the only place in town to get a decent meal probably didn't hurt either. It was built with three sides forming a horseshoe, the fourth side being the place where all the liquor bottles were stored, along with the cash register, and the tap beer. Bar stools surrounded the horseshoe. There were no tables. A kitchen was in back and another room off that. The other room turned out to be the Friday night meeting place for those who wanted to play a little poker after work. It seemed to always be full, with maybe six men sitting around a massive solid oak table, sweating away their week's wages.

I took a stool and ordered a tap beer, Olympia, very cold and very good. I searched the menu and settled for a hamburger and fries. I had a second beer while waiting for the cook to prepare my order. There weren't many people in the bar at this time of day. The waitress, a short, grandmotherly-looking woman with blue hair, introduced herself as May, and asked the usual questions about where I was from and had I ever been to Washington before. I wondered how many times she had repeated that scene and those same questions. I doubted she would remember the information I gave her but she was a kind person and I quickly discovered her type was in short supply in Strasborg.

My food arrived and I could see why Ben had recommended the place. The burger was all beef and stuck into a generous bun, smothered with mustard and pickles. A large slice of the sweetest tasting onion I had ever eaten accompanied it. The fries still had part of their skin on, but they were home sliced, not the pre-frozen kind restaurants usually serve. They were lightly salted and piping hot.

I decided against another beer, but stayed a few minutes to visit with May and talk about the cannery. I paid my tab, left a nice tip and headed back to the bunkhouse. Tomorrow I would sign up in the office for Social Security, buy a meal ticket and begin work.

The air was cool and offered a welcome respite from the dry heat that had assaulted me just a short while earlier. As I walked back to the bunkhouse I felt bone tired. I took my shoes off and settled back on my bunk as soon as I got inside. I was just dozing off, when the walls began to shake and the bunk next to mine began to dance. A train was passing by and I hoped this wasn't a nightly run. I pulled my pillow over my head and tried to go to sleep. Oklahoma was a long way off and once again I found myself wondering if my mother was right. I drifted into a fitful sleep full of dreams of long, warm, summer nights, a beautiful girl by my side and the promise of a future full of hope. All too soon those dreams would become nightmares.

CHAPTER III

"You're going to do what?" my mother asked, stopping her glass of iced tea halfway to her mouth.

"I'm going to Washington to work this summer," I answered with a calmness that I didn't feel. I was dreading the discussion that I knew would follow when I made my announcement.

"Why?" she demanded to know.

"Because I need a job so I can go back to college in the fall," I carefully explained as I gave my rehearsed speech.

"But you don't have to go all the way to Washington, do you?" she asked.

"Probably not," I admitted. "But the pay is better than I can get anywhere around here. Besides, I've never been to Washington and I want to go."

"I've never been to Washington either," she countered. "And I don't want to go now." To her, the idea of going to Washington was just as probable as going to the moon. "You could probably get a job at Safeway or one of the other grocery stores," she argued. "You don't know anyone there, how will you get up there, that costs money you know." She had an argument for everything.

"Look," I said wearily, "I know I don't know anyone, that's part of the reason I want to go. I want to meet other people from other places. I don't want to go my whole life without meeting anyone outside of this town or Oklahoma. I'll have to leave here someday so I might as well find out now what the rest of the world is like, don't you think?"

"No," she said promptly. "You will have plenty of time to do that after you graduate from college." The idea that one could do both was as foreign to her as a Parisian in the small town we lived in.

"Mom," I said as patiently as I could, "that's the whole point, I can't wait until I graduate to find out how the rest of the world lives."

"But it could be dangerous, you don't know anyone. How will you live with people you don't even know?" Her imagination was now running wild with thoughts of what kind of harm I could fall victim to.

"I have already told you, Mom," I explained as patiently as I could. "I will have to someday live and work with people I have never met so this could be a great opportunity. And as for living arrangements everyone lives in a bunkhouse so I don't have to find a place to live. It's already taken care of." I knew as soon as I said that it was the wrong thing to say.

"A bunk house," she cried, "You don't know what kind of people you will find in those places. You could get robbed, or worse yet murdered." She was really on a roll now and I could tell no amount of talking was going to convince her.

"Mom," I said, as firmly as I could, "I lived in a dormitory with two hundred other guys at college and not a single one of them was murdered."

She glared at me. "That was different," she said. "Those boys were there to get an education and not out taking dope and Lord knows what else."

It was a good thing my mother never met some of the guys living in my dorm, I thought, *or I probably would not have had that opportunity either.* I could imagine her reaction to "Crazy Joe," who lived just three doors down and was fond of talking to the light bulbs in the narrow hallways in the early hours of the morning. Joe, who recited incantations in an unknown tongue before eating, "Crazy Joe" could clear the cafeteria faster than the bad meatloaf the cooks served twice a week. Joe also liked to play basketball for hours in the gymnasium until he worked up a lather like a horse running in the Kentucky Derby. Then he would go in and put on his black wool suit and still wearing his white sweat socks and tennis shoes go to the basketball games. There were always plenty of empty seats near Joe.

Or maybe she would have liked Bob, from Michigan, who after a night of drinking would go into the nearest diner, have the largest, most expensive breakfast on the menu, and then announce he had no money to pay for it. Or perhaps I should have introduced her to the two Neo-Nazis who lived next door. Or better yet, I should have told her about the avowed communists on campus. She would really have flipped to know they weren't students at all, but professors of political science and English.

My mother's view of the world had not changed much and I was not going to convince her otherwise. I really didn't feel like trying. To tell the truth I wasn't sure I wanted to change her naiveté about certain thing such as what really was happening on college campuses in the early Sixties.

My mother was born and had lived in the same small town of Thompson's Valley all of her life. To her, life was a simple equation. Most people were good and did what was right, especially those from Thompson's Valley and other small towns like it. Some people were bad, mainly those from large cities who wouldn't hesitate to take advantage of a stranger. I never had the heart to ask her how strangers were treated in Thompson's Valley. She probably would have said there were no strangers there since everyone knew everyone else and perhaps she was right. After all, how many strangers can there be in a town of seven thousand.

Thompson's Valley was nestled on the banks of the Washita River, an area with rich farmland and abundant gas and oil. Both resources had made several members of the community wealthy by anyone's standards. Unfortunately we were not among those in this group. It was a beautiful little town with cobblestone streets and giant Oaks lining both sides of the major street coming into the city. In the spring and early summer one could drive a car for many blocks down that street with the Oaks forming a canopy overhead. The scent of honeysuckle and flowering crab apple is something I still remembered. While my mother's perception of the community was one that believed everyone was treated equally, I knew better.

In the Forties and Fifties, before the popularity of wall-to-wall carpeting, air conditioning and polyester, a staple in every household was a broom. A real broom that was made from real broomcorn, not polyester and synthetic fibers like today's models.

Broomcorn was part of the legacy of Thompson's Valley and surrounding communities. While corn, wheat and oats were grown in the area, it was this odd hybrid that drove the economy for many years in the whole area. Broomcorn was the staple crop in the valley and indeed one of the neighboring towns billed itself for years as the broomcorn capitol of the world. The straw that was used to make seventy percent of the brooms in the United States came from the county in which Thompson's Valley was located.

Harvesting the broomcorn was without doubt the hottest, most miserable job in the world. If there is a hell on earth it must be a broomcorn field. Broomcorn, you see, reacts on human skin much like a stinging nettle. A slap across the arm or neck with a stalk of broomcorn is like having a thousand ants biting you at the same time. If you are allergic to it you break out in great red welts that itch for hours. I have seen men and women with eyes swollen nearly shut during the harvest and yet they continued to cut the corn.

It was under these conditions that I first witnessed the difference in how people were treated and really became aware of the differences between just being poor and living in poverty. It was how I first became aware of the lengths to which people would go to provide for their families.

Each year when the harvest began, usually late June or early July, Thompson's Valley and all of the county would swell in population as migrant workers came up from Texas and Mexico to work in the fields. The first in the fields would be the breakers as they were known. Usually, they were older men who had worked for years in the harvest. They would enter the rows of corn and break the stalks behind their backs, first the left, then the right. In the process they would form a table on which the cut corn would be placed in bundles.

After the field was broken the "johnnies" would enter the field to do the actual cutting. I never knew why these workers were called johnnies and I am not sure anyone else did but it was a name that everyone understood. The johnnies used a short wide blade knife, curved at the end, to cut the corn to lengths of about three feet. The bundles were placed on the tables where they would be picked up by other workers and taken to the threshing machine. Whole families were often hired to work as johnnies. Men and women and often children as young as twelve were allowed to work in these miserable conditions. Many of the women took great pride in the fact that they could stay up with the men in cutting the corn. If you were twelve years old and big for your age you were old enough to try your hand as a johnnie.

With temperatures often over one hundred degrees and with humidity that nearly matched it these workers would work from sunrise to sunset and cut several acres of ground a day. Many were allergic to the corn and clothed themselves in long sleeved shirts with bandannas tied around their neck to prevent the seeds and chaff from going down their collars. In the sweltering Oklahoma sun it was not uncommon to see people suffer heat exhaustion and being helped from the fields.

Children younger than twelve were often involved in the process of threshing the corn. After the heads of corn were run through the thresher to remove as much of the stinging seeds as possible the last step was to gather them in bundles and tap the ends on a barrel to remove any remaining seeds. They were then handed to a worker who laid them out on slats in an open shed to dry. These workers were called ants and were usually paid about seventy-five cents an hour for their labor. No one seemed to mind that children were working around heavy, dangerous machinery with open belts, gears and pulleys that could rip an arm off a careless worker. It was not uncommon to see older men missing fingers or a whole arm who had lost it as a youth in a thoughtless moment to one of the monstrous threshing machines.

Since many of the workers were migrants they could usually be found camping under the bridges of the Washita River, which ran through the county. Here they did their cooking over open fires while washing away the dirt and stinging bite of the broomcorn in the muddy, polluted waters of the Washita.

As long as they kept to their campsites the workers were left alone. It was understood that they would not come into the town except to pick up supplies. Occasionally some of the younger men would sneak into town on a Saturday night in search of a little excitement. They were promptly rounded up and sent back to their camps. Fraternization with the locals, especially females, was not looked upon favorably by the police and community. I couldn't imagine what kind of excitement they hoped to find in Thompson's Valley, but whatever it was must have been better than what I thought to be a miserable existence.

In spite of what I perceived to be a wretched life most of the migrants seemed to enjoy themselves and the work they were doing. On occasion my friends and I would wander down at night to one of the camps in hopes of catching a glimpse of the young girls bathing in the river. We were never so fortunate. I marveled at the happy go lucky attitude of the group as loud and boisterous singing, crying babies and barking dogs punctuated the dark humid nights along the river banks. Sometimes I found myself wondering if maybe they weren't the lucky ones. They seemed to have found a way to be happy despite the great odds against them.

By the mid-Sixties, broomcorn was hardly produced in the county as manufacturers found a cheaper alternative with their synthetic fibers for brooms. Farmers began planting soybeans and other crops in what had been broomcorn fields. It was a passing lamented by some who had worked the fields every summer for years, but to most who labored in the hot Oklahoma sun I am sure it was an era they were glad to see end. My own father worked in the fields for many of his friends and neighbors. One of the things he gave me shortly before his death was a "johnnie" knife, the handle still wrapped in cloth and tape to prevent blisters. I am not sure why he gave it to me, but probably to remind me that all things and life as we know it comes to an end with little we can do to prevent the first, and nothing we can do to prevent the second.

Thompson's Valley, like all communities large and small had its prejudices and biases. Enlightment, acceptance and a sense of fair play are qualities not exclusively the domain of any part of the country nor group of people.

Still, all in all, Thompson's Valley was not a bad place to grow up, even if you were poor like I was. Like most small towns in the '50s, its citizens could leave for work, for church or simply to run an errand without having to lock their doors. Children played in the streets, the parks and chased lightning bugs on warm summer nights secure in the knowledge that they had no enemies or anyone wanting to hurt them. It was small enough so that if you were a decent athlete and halfway intelligent you were accepted by those who ran the school and community.

Those two qualities also generally meant you could date one of the better-looking and more popular girls, which I did. This was especially true if the girl happened to be Catholic, which was a rarity in rural Oklahoma. While Catholics were accepted and it was ok to be friends with them, most parents didn't want their sons and daughters dating one. In the Baptist Bible Belt, such a union would have been considered a mixed marriage, if it ever got that far.

So I dated Nancy and discovered something about religious prejudice along with all of the other hang-ups with which people burden themselves and their children.

I watched prejudice prevail, as she was first not chosen as football queen, then later basketball. These were positions of the highest honor to be bestowed upon a girl in any school. To a great degree they remain that way today, especially in the small towns where sports are a way of life as much as religion and work.

It was difficult for me to understand this kind of bias directed towards students, particularly since Nancy and her family always attended the games. I wasn't chosen as captain of either team either, but then neither was any of our black athletes. So while I wasn't Catholic or black, I was poor. Perhaps that was worse than being either, because there were more of us than them.

While Thompson's Valley was as good as any place to grow up and probably better than most, it was not a place I missed whenever I left for college. I was determined not to spend another summer there. Whatever fate awaited me on the road or in Strasborg I was sure it would be better than another summer at home.

I didn't have the courage, however, to tell my mother that I planned to hitchhike the seventeen hundred miles to Strasborg. Instead I took the coward's way out and told her I would take the bus. It was only a partial lie, as I actually did ride it the one hundred and eighty miles from Thompson's Valley to Adam's City, where I was to meet up with Pat.

CHAPTER IV

Somebody was kicking my bunk. I thought at first I was dreaming, but then I saw the shadowy figure of Bunkhouse Joe still in his long johns. He was standing at my feet. The ever-present bottle of Jim Beam was already in his hand and I wondered what kind of morning could be so bad that he had to start it with a drink of whiskey.

"Wake up," he croaked between kicks, "time to get up."

"What time is it?" I managed to ask between kicks.

"Time to get up," he said, as he went to the next bunk and started kicking it.

I was afraid to ask, but soon found out that this was apparently his only function as bunkhouse supervisor. He seemed to take a perverse pleasure in this morning ritual. In the months that I was working at the factory he never failed to perform this solitary task, regardless of the condition he had been in a few hours earlier. If nothing else, he was reliable.

Since I didn't go to work until the next day, I didn't see what the hurry was, but Joe was adamant that everyone be up at five o'clock. People had been arriving throughout the night and there was a lot of grumbling from those who had only been in bed a couple of hours.

I rolled out from beneath the warm covers reluctantly. The air was chilly and my jeans were cool as I slipped them on. Other men were being roused in the same fashion as I had been awakened.

"Knock it off, you old bastard," men mumbled as Joe continued his rounds. It was obvious from the familiarity directed at Joe that some of them had worked at the cannery before. They pleaded for him to cease his assault on their bunks but Bunkhouse Joe just kept kicking and laughing.

Those men who had selected bunks as far away from Joe as possible were familiar with his morning ritual. There were about a dozen men now sleepily rising and lighting cigarettes or heading off to the showers. I grabbed my shaving kit and headed to the lavatories. While I was shaving, a dark complexioned fellow with short wiry hair came in and set his razor down on the sink next to mine. He then stuck out his hand and introduced himself.

"Abel Hassim," he said.

"Mark James," I replied, shaking his hand.

"First year here?" he inquired.

"Yeah," I answered, "How about you?"

"No, I was here last year," he replied. "It's the pits, but it's a job for the summer. This way you can get in a lot of hours anyway."

"I guess so," I agreed, not knowing what else to say.

Hassim was a Syrian and would be a senior at Washington State University that fall. It turned out that he was one of the hardest working, quietest guys on the crew. I later found out that he was one of the ones you wanted on your side when choosing up teams for just about anything, and that was to include covering you in a fight. He was majoring in electrical engineering and was both incredibly bright and willing to work hard for his chance at landing a job in the United States.

I finished my shave, ran a comb through my hair and headed to the mess hall. It was a long, low bungalow building that sat just outside the entrance to the plant. It lacked air conditioning but the sides were mostly covered in fine screening to let what little air there was circulate. Four rows of long tables with folding chairs filled the dining area. I grabbed a tray and headed through the breakfast line. The coffee was weak, the eggs were cooked too long and the bacon not long enough. It was, unfortunately, a sign of things to come. I recalled Ben's admonition about the food.

Other men were drifting into the kitchen, exchanging handshakes, renewing acquaintances and yelling at Bert, the cook.

"You still using them powdered eggs? Still putting saltpeter in the coffee, Bert? Hey, Bert, where's your good looking wife and daughters?" They all wanted to know. I was reminded of the warning from Ben about staying away from Bert's daughters but this morning he was the only one in the kitchen.

He took their ribbing good-naturedly, grinning throughout the friendly bantering going on.

I had a second cup of the weak coffee and tried to wake up. The mess hall was now nearly full of men, ranging in age from about eighteen to around twenty-five I guessed. Most of them seemed to know someone, as greetings and handshakes were exchanged and questions were asked about how the past year of school turned out and if they were going back.

The mess hall was segregated by strict racial lines that were apparently understood by all the returning workers. At one end of the dining room, a group of Mexicans occupied two long tables and kept a constant chatter of Spanish going, punctuated with punches to the shoulders or backs. They frequently exchanged piercing glances with the rest of the men in the mess hall. It was impossible to interpret any of their conversation even though I had just finished my second year of Spanish. I gathered from the smoldering looks they cast at some of the men and the hilarious laughter that followed that some of the workers were the butt of a private joke among the group.

The rest of the room was apparently divided into two groups. One group was made up of new guys like myself, and the regulars or old-timers, who were back for a second, third, or fourth season in the factory.

I was full of weak coffee, so I left the place and walked over to the main office to take care of registration. There were only a few men there and a short, fat, gray-haired woman gave me several sheets of paper and a pen. She then motioned me to take a seat at a table. She didn't even ask what I was doing there; apparently there was no other reason for anyone to be in the office, unless he or she was there to work.

I filled in the personal data sheet: weight, height, and so forth, who to notify in case of accident, an always ominous part of any application, and all the rest of the impersonal questions that a sheet of paper can demand.

After reading it over once, I took it back to the short, fat, gray-haired lady. She read it over once over the top of her bifocal glasses and put a card in an old manual Olivetti typewriter. Modernization, in the form of electric typewriters, had not yet hit Strasborg.

She asked, without looking up, "Do you want the life insurance policy?"

Another ominous thought. "Yeah, I guess so," I responded. Someone might as well benefit if anything happened to me, I figured.

"Beneficiary?" she questioned.

"What?" I said.

"Beneficiary, you know, who do you want to get the insurance money in case something happens to you?" She was eyeing me over the top of her glasses, which were perched so low on her nose I thought they might slip off at any minute.

I thought about it for a moment and then gave her the name of my parents. Who else would I be leaving anything to at the age of twenty-one, I wondered to myself.

"Do you want us to save your checks 'till the end of the season?" she continued.

"No, thanks, I'll pick them up payday," I told her.

I found out later that if they kept your checks until the end of the harvest, they didn't really put them away for you. Instead, they just gave you one big check at the end of the season and that way the company got to use your money for the entire three months you worked. Anyway, there were several men who had them keep their checks until they quit because they didn't trust themselves with the money. Some were afraid they would just lose it each week at a poker game and, in fact, some did just that. Others just ended up drinking theirs away or losing it on the scratch games and punch cards at the local American Legion hall. I wanted to see the money in my hands however. Even though I would be sending each check home for deposit so it would be there for me to pay my tuition in the fall I liked knowing it was in my hands.

"Do you want a meal ticket?" the lady interrupted my thoughts.

I wondered if she would notice if I just said, "Mind your own damn business, why don't you?"

Instead, I said, "I suppose so." I knew since there wasn't any place else to get breakfast at five-thirty in the morning, I better have something to eat before I started my six-hour shift before lunch.

"Sign here," she indicated, ripping the card out of the old Olivetti.

I did so without any questions. She didn't seem to be the sort of person who was used to having her authority questioned.

I did as I was told, not really even taking time to read the information, which she had typed on the five-by-eight card.

"Be here tomorrow morning at five-forty-five and someone will show you your assignment," she said, still not looking up, but already getting the next card into the typewriter.

The way she said, "Be here at five-forty-five," made me feel like she was pronouncing my execution date.

Since it was early, I walked back to the bunkhouse, but no one was there. I decided I might as well go into town and see if anything was happening. I soon discovered that nothing much ever happened in Strasborg.

I walked the quarter mile into town under a bright, warm sun that quickly took away the early morning chill. It was early spring in Strasborg and an occasional breeze caused the leaves to flutter gently on the trees that lined the banks of the little stream that ran by the edge of town. There was a pleasant but unfamiliar smell in the air, which I discovered, came from the many different crops grown in the valley. In addition to the peas, many fruits and vegetables were produced in the area. The town seemed to be deserted when I reached

Main Street as I saw no one in sight. I walked up one side of the street, looking in the store windows: a cafe, a hardware store, what I thought was a plumbing shop. Then across the street, a bar, a junk shop, a small grocery store, an old movie theater with a life size poster of Gordon Macrae announcing *Oklahoma* to be shown next week.

I was homesick, and wondered what my parents were doing at that very moment. I felt the sudden urge to call them or perhaps Nancy, whom I hadn't seen in almost two years. We had both decided to attend different colleges after our graduation from high school and from what I heard from mutual friends she was doing very well. I, on the other hand, had not made a great record for myself in the two years since she had decided to end our relationship. I abandoned the thought of calling her since I did not handle rejection very well.

Instead, I walked down to the Palm Club hoping it might be open and I could visit with May. The doors were closed and a sign said, "Open at nine o'clock." Then I remembered the other bar I had passed. I turned around and headed in that direction.

It was called the Twenty-One Club, never to be confused with the one in New York by the same name. It was open and I apparently was the first customer. Three hours later, I was still the first and only customer.

The barkeep was a shuffling, old, white-haired gentleman of about seventy who had once lived in Adam's City, Oklahoma. I made a mental note to tell Pat, since that was his hometown. I knew he would be down to visit and tell lies. The old man was excited about the movie coming to town and kept saying how he wanted to see if Oklahoma was still like he remembered it when he lived there. I didn't have the heart to tell him that it wasn't filmed in Oklahoma at all but on some movie studio lot. He asked if I wanted a beer, except he pronounced it "bea." He kept an unlit cigar clamped between his false teeth and I never once saw him take it out the whole time I was there.

I drank about six Olympias and found I was developing a taste for the stuff. I played pool by myself on a beautiful, antique billiard table from which I carefully cleaned what must have been a month's worth of dust. The old man shuffled and talked about the pea crop. I talked about Oklahoma, which I knew something about, and the old man kept asking questions. He hadn't been back in forty years, but he kept asking me if I knew people that he called by name. I tried to explain that Oklahoma was considerably bigger than he must recall.

I grew tired of playing pool by myself, so I said goodbye to the old gent and walked over to the Palm Club. It was open this time and most of the stools were occupied by people having lunch or just a beer. I had a hamburger with extra onions, French fries and another Olympia. The hamburger was just as good as I remembered from the night before. Apparently some things are just as good as you remember them to be.

I finished my meal and started the walk back when I decided to stop at a small grocery store and buy a couple of magazines to help pass the time. When I arrived at the bunkhouse there were more late arrivals coming in, which raised the ire of Bunkhouse Joe for causing him to have to crawl out of his cot to issue them bedding.

Pat arrived about six o'clock and demanded to know why the hell I didn't meet him in Colorado Springs, the way we had agreed. I made up some excuse about catching a ride all the way to Salt Lake and then on to Boise. I never told him about Leigh. Some things I didn't want to share and that was one memory I intended to keep to myself for a while.

Pat was going to be working the night shift because it paid a dime more per hour. We caught up on the rest of our travel experiences, knowing that we would probably not be seeing each other very often during the harvest as I would be arriving for work just as he was leaving.

I skipped supper, read the magazines, and went to bed early and was sound asleep when my bunk began to dance and I awoke. *Damn train,* I thought to myself.

Someone was kicking my bunk, but this time I knew what was happening. I crawled out from beneath the blankets and beat everyone to the shower room. I skipped shaving, just splashing cold water on my face and combing my hair.

The air was cold at that time of the morning and I was glad for my Levi jacket. Strasborg was really a desert so the nights could get very cold after the hot days of summer. The stars were still out, with only a faint glimmer in the east. It was going to be a long day if I could believe everything that I had been hearing from the veterans who were returning.

About fifty of us assembled at the timekeeper's office and waited for our name to be read. We were then given our job assignment. My name, along with about ten others, was called and we were told that we would be crate loaders, the lowest rung on the factory level. It was apparently the place where all new employees started to work. It was also the hardest and the most boring job in the plant. Some of the men who were returning for their second or third year were assigned to relatively easy jobs as supervisors or what was laughingly called quality control. Except for a job as a field hand a crate loader was as menial a job a worker could have.

Only Mexicans were assigned to the field hand work. I never saw any blacks working in any capacity while I was at Strasborg. The Mexicans went to work at five o'clock I found out later. They had to leave an hour early to get to the fields, so they could be on the job at six. I also found out later that they were not paid for this extra hour they had to work. It was considered to be part of their job. The mornings were still cold at that hour and their fingers must have been frozen as they picked and sorted the peas and vines. Although machines did most of the picking, the Mexicans had to untangle the vines and pick anything the machines left behind.

Later on, the sun turned the fields unmercifully hot. The giant pea picking machines created clouds of thick dust that enveloped the land and the workers. In fact, the Mexicans would leave layers of it on the shower floor turning the surface into slick ribbons of white grease. We always tried to beat them to the bunkhouse after work, so we could shower before they arrived. I wondered how they could breathe at all in the dust created by the machines. None of them wore masks the way men in the wheat elevators did back in Oklahoma. I would occasionally see one with a scarf tied around his face, but it was always caked with dirt from the dust and their own sweat. The dust, fertilizer and insecticide sprayed on the peas must have taken a terrible toll on their lungs after a season in the fields. In so many ways they reminded me of the broomcorn johnnies that worked the fields back home. Perhaps ten years earlier they would have been part of the migrant laborers working the fields in Thompson's Valley.

Despite their miserable jobs, they seemed to be a happy bunch, chattering and laughing all the time, staying up late, drinking beer and smoking the foulest smelling cigarettes imaginable. I didn't spend a lot of time thinking about them however, since my own job kept me preoccupied.

One day I decided to ask our foreman why none of them worked in the plant. I might as well have asked why none of the popes were Methodist. He looked at me and replied mater-of-factly, "They're Mexicans, that's why. They'll do anything for a buck."

I didn't ask any more questions about other peoples' jobs after that, since I had no desire to join the Mexicans in the fields.

A crate loader, as I said, was the beginning and lowest position in the factory. It required constant movement, although you never had to move more than two feet in any direction. In fact, a worker couldn't move more than that and still be at his station.

The peas were first washed after arriving from the fields and then dumped into a chute, which carried them into giant funnel shaped hoppers. From there, they were fed into another funnel and the cans were carried on an assembly line. Once the cans started moving, the peas flowed from the funnel and filled each can. Then they were sealed and fed onto another line, where they were loaded on crates and taken to giant cookers.

I never thought about peas being cooked while in the can, but I guess, for sanitary reasons, it was logical. Although, I can't say the owners were overly concerned about cleanliness, judging from some of the things that made it into the cans and hoppers. I saw people with their hands in the hoppers constantly picking out handfuls of peas and eating them like peanuts. I always thought of Ben and what he had said about the women of Strasborg when I saw one of them with a handful of peas. They tasted something like a nut with a slightly sweet taste before cooking. Other times, I saw lifesavers, chewing gum and some items I couldn't identify at all in the hoppers. All would end up in someone's can of peas for dinner.

The peas came down the assembly line at the rate of fifty-four a minute for the regular size cans and seventy-two a minute for the smaller ones. The pace was demanding and it was virtually impossible to keep up with production. When the cans began to pile up and started jamming the assembly line the workers would simply shove a huge armload off the line onto the floor. The men who operated the cookers then had to come over, pick up the fallen cans, and see that they were placed back on the assembly line. This gave the crater loaders time to use the empty conveyor space and get caught up.

Crate loaders stood at the end of the assembly line, next to a raised platform. A large iron crate was pushed up to work stations on small railroad tracks and then over a hoist on the floor. With one hand the workers operated a lever, which raised the bottom of the crate level with your station and then placed an iron pallet on top. With the other hand loaders held a Y-shaped piece of steel, with which he scooped and raked the cans into the crate. When one level was full, workers pulled the lever and lowered the top about ten inches, placed another pallet on top of the cans and kept scooping. People had to learn to do this while the cans kept coming at their steady rate of fifty-four or seventy-two a minute. It was boring, repetitious work that never gave the operators a chance to look up and almost no chance to talk with any of the other workers.

The work numbed my shoulders and hands and made my legs feel as if they were set in concrete after a twelve-hour shift. My back ached constantly from the strain of scooping the cans from my right side to my left onto the carts. The leather gloves I wore were worn through the first week and did little to prevent large blisters from appearing on my "scooping" hand. By the end of summer my right arm was about an inch larger than my left since it was the one I used to load the peas on the crate. Work began promptly at six in the morning and ended at six at night when we handed our scoop to night replacements. There was no such thing as a coffee break and only thirty minutes for lunch, which usually consisted of Bert's meat loaf or chili. I spent most of the lunch break dreaming of a hamburger from the Palm Club or hoping for a malfunction in equipment, which might give us a break.

When the crates were loaded, a process that took about seventeen minutes, they were pulled off the hoist onto small adjoining railroad tracks and shoved into the giant ovens for cooking. Fully loaded, they weighed close to fifteen hundred pounds. It would have been impossible to move them without the tracks they rested on. While a loaders job was not an easy one it meant the workers at least got some rest while the crates were being filled.

The ovens were about thirty feet long and about twenty feet in circumference. They could hold eight of the loaded crates. After the peas were quick cooked and sterilized in their cans, cool water was pumped into the cookers to cool the crates. They were then removed and the process repeated. The heating and then the cooling of the peas meant the workroom was constantly filled with steam, which only added to the discomfort. At times I felt like I was trying to breath under water. The night workers made thirty-five cents more per hour. Those men working the freezer sections made another dime more. Whatever shift a person worked, it was long, hot and boring unless of course you worked the freezers where it was long, cold and boring. The combination of steam, heat and the hot machinery sometimes raised the temperature to one hundred and twenty degrees. I guess no one had ever thought of installing fans to circulate air since I never saw one in any of the buildings except the offices. It probably wasn't done because it would have cost too much money.

I heard a lot of stories about how the pressure cookers had blown at one time and plastered some crate loaders against the back wall. We worked directly in front of them, so it was not a reassuring story. A two thousand pound steel door blown off its hinges would have wiped out half the work force in the plant. Rumor had it that at least once; a cooker had gone into the ovens to adjust a crate and was locked in. When they opened it to remove the peas all they found was a skeleton, since the steam had literally cooked him to death. True or not, I was not amused. Occasionally, the steam would build up to excessive levels in the cookers and then a low piercing whistle would begin just like a teakettle when the water is boiling. Whenever that happened, the workers would throw down their scoops and run like hell for the exits. The result was chaos, of course, with peas piling up on the assembly line and flying everywhere. Management, needless to say got furious when this happened, because it delayed the work for a few minutes. Time down, meant lost money. Apparently, safety was not a big concern for those who worked in the offices. Women usually worked the assembly lines and kept the cans flowing, seeing to it that the lids were sealed and nothing clogged up the hoppers. Most of them were fat and most of them were ugly. Most of them also put out, a fact which made their looks a lot easier to deal with. Besides, when you're in Strasborg, Washington you could not be particular.

There was one kid in the bunkhouse, named Stan, about eighteen years old. Stan came from Ohio. He let it slip one day that he was still a virgin. Everyone immediately set out to correct this unfortunate situation.

Concerned as we were about his state, we immediately arranged for him to have a date with one of the assembly line girls. We selected a slightly overweight girl, named Becky, who, word had it, not only put out, but also was a first class nympho.

The date was arranged for after work one Saturday night. Becky would pick up Stan, since she had a 1960 Corvair, and they would probably go to Walla Walla for a drive-in-movie. We coached Stan all week on what to say and do. You would have thought him to be the star quarterback and us the coaches getting him pumped up for the big game.

"Don't ask for it, don't rush it, get her to let you feel her tits first." Something we had all been assured would be no problem with Becky, if the rumors about her nymphomania were true. Those of us who had taken an interest in Stan's dilemma offered far too much advice. Most of it I am confident was bad and did nothing to ease his fears.

The poor guy didn't know what he should do and I began to wonder if we perhaps were being unkind. After all, we were sending a child into what could not exactly be called virgin territory. As the week progressed it became difficult to tell who was more excited, Stan or the guys in the bunkhouse.

Saturday night finally arrived and I believe it was fair to say that no person had ever had as much attention as we devoted to Stan that week. Like a matador going into the bullring, we saw to it that he shaved twice, showered for twenty minutes, had clean clothes to wear. We especially made sure that his underwear was clean, even though we didn't expect him to be in them very long given his date's reputation. Everything was done to make him presentable in his sacrificial role.

Becky would arrive at eight o'clock. We made him buy a bottle of vodka, which we assured him would probably not be necessary if Becky was as easy as rumor had it. Nothing was to be overlooked, however, as we all felt like parents protecting their child.

Eight o'clock finally arrived and Becky pulled up to the bunkhouse in her brown Corvair. It reminded me of a scene from Christmas at Grandma's house, as ten people began shouting, "She's here, she's here, get ready, Stan." You would have thought he was going to get laid right on the bunkhouse floor, something that he or anyone else could probably have accomplished with the willing Becky. Somehow, we got him loaded into the Corvair and off they went, the virgin being offered up for sacrifice.

We settled back to await Stan's return. We didn't have to wait long.

Hardly an hour had passed and most of the men had gone into town to drink or play poker in the back room of the Palm Club. A few of us were playing nickel, dime, quarter poker on one of the bunks, when the door burst open and a wild-eyed, sweaty Stan, wearing only his underwear, dashed straight for his bunk.

We were astonished. All of us were taken aback for a moment. No one spoke. Then someone giggled, then a laugh, more laughter, and then a madhouse as we rushed to Stan's bunk to hear the juicy details.

"How was it?" a half-dozen voices wanted to know in unison.

"Was it as good as I've heard?" Someone asked.

"How about it Stan? Let's hear all about it," we pleaded with him.

From underneath his blanket, a muffled voice came. "Don't let her in the bunkhouse."

"What?" We all said together, not believing what we were hearing from our fallen warrior.

"Don't let her in," came from beneath the blanket again, now in a pleading tone that seemed to be on the verge of hysteria.

A car was circling the bunkhouse, horn blaring, lights blinking. Someone was yelling, a girl's voice, "Come on out an' play, Stan." We heard Becky's pleading cry for him to come back and finish the job he had started, but our man Stan was determined to stay exactly where he was.

We were rolling on the floor, crying from laughing so hard.

Finally, Becky left and an anxious Stan peered out from beneath his covers.

With a little coaxing, we finally got his story. The stories about Becky and her sexual appetite were evidently true.

The road behind the bunkhouse crossed the railroad tracks and followed the mountain for a distance, before diverging off into several smaller trails. Evidently, Becky had no interest in the drive-in-movie or even the vodka. No indeed, not one to waste time, our girl Becky had immediately set out on one of the trails with our friend Stan, with the intention of releasing him of his terrible burden. For Stan it was too much, too soon.

We were ashamed of ourselves. We had thrown a child into man's play, a Christian to the lions, a virgin to the savages. Becky had succeeded in removing Stan's shirt, shoes, socks and Levis, but just when the moment of truth had almost arrived, our man Stan had bolted from the arms of his partner and left her both waiting and wanting. And, I would imagine, a little startled.

Stan had run all the way to the bunkhouse, clad only in his Fruit of the Looms.

Realizing that we had too much at stake in this venture, we swore to Stan and ourselves that no one should ever know the truth about that night. So Stan's secret was safe and, apparently, so was his virginity. At least for that summer.

CHAPTER V

The work at the cannery quickly became drudgery. The constant repetition of raking the cans off the table onto the crates made my arms ache from shoulder to fingertip. As soon as one blister would break on my hand another more painful one would appear. The room was unbearably hot with steam and heat, and the noise from the machines deafening. Still, we kept at it from six to six, with our thirty minutes off for lunch. Almost daily, someone passed out from heat exhaustion. More and more of the men left for home, giving up and simply walking out one day and not returning the next. The managers and foremen came around and offered time and a half for those who were willing to work an extra two or three hours beyond their regular shift. There were no takers. As soon as work was over we headed for the bunkhouse and a long cold shower, which was refreshing after the heat and steam of the workroom. Then it was into town for a hamburger at the Palm Club, or to the cafeteria for some of Bert's bad food when we were too exhausted to do anything else.

One day, at the end of my shift, the foreman came around and told us we would have the next two days off while we waited for a field of peas to ripen. We yelled, shook hands, and threw our hats in the air.

Two whole days off, I thought. *Time to go into Walla Walla, where the good-looking women lived. Time to really get drunk and not worry about your head falling off the next day.* Some of the men even made plans to go to Spokane.

I planned to get to Walla Walla and relax. I could get drunk anytime without having to spend my free time on the road hitchhiking again.

I caught a ride, early the next morning with one of the guys who had enough and was going home to Oregon. He dropped me off at the Best Western Motel, where I got a room and immediately took the longest, hottest shower that I had in weeks. With clean clothes on, I felt ready for anything.

The motel was just at the edge of town, so I walked in to see about dinner and have a look around. Everyone seemed to be outside doing business. A huge banner strung across the street declared this to be Walla Walla's annual Krazy Daze sale. Clerks were dressed in clown suits, makeup, red and white hats with balls on top, holding huge cigars in their mouths. *What people do to make a buck?* I thought. Then I thought about my own job. Someone could say the same about me.

I walked up the street for several blocks, looking at the merchandise: bright colored Bermuda shorts, Hawaiian shirts, towels, waste baskets, jewelry. All of it set outside, piled high on tables that lined the sidewalk. Women and men were rummaging through stacks, hoping to find an overlooked bargain.

I crossed the street and started back in the direction from which I had been walking. I passed a store with tables piled high with cowboy boots and belts with turquoise buckles and names stamped in the back. If your name wasn't John, Joe, Bill or Bob you were out of luck.

It was almost five o'clock and clerks were beginning to haul the merchandise back inside. Some were making reduced sale signs for tomorrow's onslaught. I was debating a pair of lizard skin boots when she spoke.

"Hi, I'm Debbie, can I help you?"

She was beautiful. The Raggedy Ann costume couldn't hide the sparkle in her eyes. The red mop for hair only accented her soft brown skin. The painted freckles called attention to lips that were full and bright red. She had a slightly tilted nose just like a real Raggedy Ann doll. I knew I was about to become the owner of a pair of genuine Tony Lama lizard skin boots.

"Like those boots?" Raggedy Ann spoke. "Those are real lizard skin, not fake leather, you know."

Her voice, a lilting, precocious mixture of laughter and husky whisper, carried through the noisy hum of shoppers.

"Yes," I stammered, "they seem nice enough."

"What's your size?" She wanted to know.

"Size ten," I answered, "ten D."

"Bet we have a pair," she said, picking up boots and checking the insides.

"Here you go," she said, handing me a pair. "Why don't you just sit down back here and step into these." She was motioning to a bench set under a large, green umbrella, which stuck out of the middle of a table.

I didn't need to try them on, but I didn't want her to leave. "Okay," I said, "I might take an eleven in this boot though."

"We got some." She smiled, displaying a small pink tongue and perfect, small white teeth.

I took my time trying the boots on, walking, stretching, and feeling the leather. They fit like a pair of well-worn gloves.

"What is all of this," I asked, waving my hand to indicate the stores and clerks.

"Krazy Daze," she answered, like it was perfectly clear to any fool what that was. "All the merchants get rid of spring and summer merchandise in August with this big promotion. Tonight there's a rodeo and tomorrow even bigger sales with lots of contests downtown."

"What kind of contests?" I asked. I was struggling to keep the conversation going because I didn't want to leave just yet. It had been a long time since I had even seen a pretty girl let alone talk to one. My conversation with women for the past two months had been limited to May at the Palm Club, or the women who operated the hoppers.

"Oh, a dunking tank, ring toss, that kind of thing," she answered. "You plan to be around?" she asked, giving me what I took to be an encouraging smile.

"Maybe, it depends," I said as casually as I could.

"On what?" She demanded to know.

"Whether or not you'll be here."

"I have to work tomorrow," she said, in what I hoped was a disappointed tone.

"That's too bad," I answered, hoping she caught my own disappointment, which was genuine.

"But, I'm free tonight," she smiled at me showing those perfect white teeth.

There really was a God and he did answer prayers after all, I thought, as I picked up my new lizard skin boots.

"Great," I said, trying to sound as if I picked up girls and made dates with them every day. "Only problem is," I continued, "I don't have a car."

"That's no problem," she volunteered. "I do. You don't live here, do you?"

"No," I confessed, half afraid she was about to tell me to forget it. "I'm staying at the Best Western at the edge of town, room two thirty-seven."

"Good, how about if I pick you up at seven-thirty?"

"Sounds fine to me," I said, still not believing my incredible good luck. I couldn't believe that ten minutes before I didn't even know her name.

With that she sent me inside to pay for my boots and ran off to finish the day's business. I headed back to the motel. On the way I stopped at a liquor store, just before I got to the motel. I bought a pint of Jack Daniels and then, on second thought, a pint of vodka. I had no idea if she even drank, but I wanted to please and be prepared. For that matter I had no idea if she would even show up. *Hell*, I thought, *she's probably made a dozen dates today*. Probably a good way to make a sale. I wondered how many other suckers were wearing a pair of unneeded Tony Lama genuine lizard skin boots because Raggedy

Ann had smiled at them. I began to feel like a fool. By the time I got to the motel, I was convinced that I had been taken. *What an idiot,* I thought to myself. *Two months of isolation in Strasborg and I really think this girl is going out with someone she just met.*

Back in my room I mixed myself a large bourbon and water, turned on the television and sat down to brood and curse my stupidity. I couldn't believe I had let myself be played for such a fool. My new boots sat at the end of the bed, a mocking reminder of my gullibility.

I finished the bourbon, took a cold shower, mixed myself another drink and changed into clean Levis and a shirt. Just for the hell of it, I tried on the boots. They were nice, even if I didn't need them. I tried to convince myself that I was not getting my hopes too high and that I would laugh tomorrow about the joke that had been played on me.

It was seven o'clock so I switched on the television for company. Bonanza was on, a rerun I noticed. I mixed my third drink and settled back on the bed to enjoy my first night away from the bunkhouse and the realization that I didn't have to get up at five o'clock tomorrow for work.

At seven-thirty, a commercial break came on and there was a knock at my door. I knocked over my drink on the bedside table. I was acting like some sixteen year old on his first date, as I fumbled for the latch and opened the door. *Stan the Man could not have been handling things any worse than I was at the moment,* I thought.

The girl standing in my doorway had long blond hair, hanging in soft curls around her shoulders. Her eyes were ice blue and they did look like Raggedy Ann's. She didn't have freckles, but if she did, they would not have been out of place. Her lips were full and wet and when she smiled, they opened to show the small pink tongue and perfect white teeth I had seen that afternoon.

"It's me, Debbie," she laughed, as I realized I still had not said anything.

"Come in," I finally stammered, regaining some of my composure. "I guess I was expecting Raggedy Ann," I offered as a way of excuse.

"Hope you're not disappointed," she said, with a sort of half smile, half pout of those gorgeous lips.

"Not at all, how about a drink?" I indicated the bourbon and vodka on the dresser.

"Bourbon and water would be just fine," she answered, looking around the room. She even drank what I did. I took that as a good omen.

I busied myself mixing the drinks, hoping that I got the combination right and trying to steady my hand.

"So, how do you like Walla Walla?" She wanted to know.

"So far, it's been great," I answered, handing her the drink.

"By the way," she said, "I don't even know your name." I realized then that she was right. I had been so taken with her that afternoon that I had not even introduced myself.

"Mark," I said, "Mark James, from Oklahoma."

"Glad to know you, Mark James from Oklahoma," she said, touching her glass to mine, which I felt, was a fairly intimate gesture. "Like I said earlier, I'm Debbie, Debbie Braxton from Walla Walla, a born native of Washington State."

We made small talk for a time while we finished our drinks, mostly about her job and mine at the cannery. She took a seat in one of the two chairs in the room while I sat on the bed. She seemed to know a great deal about the cannery and I could only guess that I wasn't the only guy she knew who was spending his summer working there.

She suggested that we go to the rodeo she had mentioned that afternoon. Although I had ridden bulls while working my way through college, I really didn't have much interest in seeing another one unless it was a big one like the Pendleton Round Up. I could tell, however, that this was a big event for her, so I tried to sound enthusiastic about going.

I was on familiar ground at rodeos. The smell of horse manure and wet leather were enough to make me a little homesick. Going to them was a natural thing to do in the summers in Oklahoma. Every small town had one between May and August and half the guys I grew up with had ridden in them.

While I bought the tickets, Debbie had grabbed two Cokes from a passing vendor and motioned me to follow her. Before leaving the room, she had slipped the bottle of Jack Daniels into her purse. Now she produced it and, pouring a little Coke out of each cup she replaced it with the bourbon. She used her finger for a swizzle stick.

She was a big rodeo fan and kept yelling like she was at a football game, screaming encouragement to the riders and ropers, swearing at the bulls and steers. She had a reaction for every action. I wondered if she was that enthusiastic about everything. The rodeo was small time and the contestant's obviously mostly local cowboys as few of them could stay aboard the horses and bulls for the required eight seconds. It really didn't matter what was happening in the arena, as I was too aware of her constant clutching of my arm or knee during a particularly tense ride.

As the last bull rider was announced, she gripped my arm and said, "Let's go and beat the crowd."

"Where?" I wanted to know.

"To Fuzzy's," she answered, already moving down the bleacher seats.

Fuzzy's turned out to be a local hangout for the rodeo crowd. It had a nice size dance floor which was nearly empty when we got there. It would soon fill with beautiful women in tight-fitting Levis and boots and men with equally tight jeans and large hats that sported everything from a single feather to nests that looked like a wildlife refuge.

"Hi, Fuzzy," Debbie spoke to a middle-aged man, wearing a neatly trimmed gray beard and short curly gray hair. He looked liked someone's favorite uncle.

"Meet my friend, Mark, from Oklahoma," she introduced me.

We shook hands as I admired Fuzzy's hat, a ten-gallon version with a coiled rattlesnake staring back at me with glass eyes. I had the distinct impression that all wildlife in Washington was on the endangered species list. Or at least, Fuzzy's list.

"Glad to meet you. Hope you enjoy your visit," he said. He had no idea how much I was enjoying myself.

Debbie selected a table near the band and drinks arrived. I never knew who took our order, but it was Jack Daniels and water, just what I always drank. I figured she must be a regular for she seemed to know everybody. As the rodeo crowd kept arriving, she waved and spoke to almost everyone who came in the door.

The band had three guitarists and a drummer. One of the guitar players also doubled on the fiddle. They were playing a two-step, their version of Bob Wills' San Antonio Rose. Without waiting for me to ask her, she took my hand and led me to the dance floor.

She was a terrific dancer and while I didn't think I was all that bad I could see that she had a lot more practice than I on the dance floor. She was light and smooth, and made even me look good. After finishing the two-step the band went into a swing dance and again she took the initiative, turning and doing twirls at just the right time. We decided to sit the next one out and headed back to our table. More of her friends kept dropping by to say hello or offering to buy us drinks. It was easy to see that she was well liked and well known. I kept wondering how a girl like her didn't have a date since most of the other people seemed to be in pairs, but I didn't question my good fortune.

About twelve-thirty, she suggested that it was time to think about heading home. In a way, I didn't want to leave, but, on the other hand, I was anxious to be alone with her. With her friends constantly stopping by our table to say hello I had hardly spoken to her. She drove me straight to the motel, all the time talking about the rodeo, the band at Fuzzy's and how much fun she had. She pulled into the parking lot of the Best Western and before I could say a word, she looked at me and said, "I'd love to come in, but it's late and I have to work tomorrow. If you still plan to be in town I'll pick you up at seven-thirty tomorrow night, if you would like. Maybe we can do something a little quieter, like a movie, if that's ok."

"That would be great," I said. I still was not accustomed to a girl being so direct and forward, but I guessed I would get used to it if I were around Debbie for very long.

Quickly she leaned over and took my face in both hands and kissed me. It was over too soon, but she was already putting the car in gear and I reluctantly got out since I could see she was serious about leaving.

"See you tomorrow," she yelled as she drove away leaving me standing in the middle of the motel parking lot.

Sleep didn't come easy that night, so I went to the coffee shop and drank coffee until two o'clock, which didn't help either.

The next morning, I had just a slight headache, which reminded me of how much whiskey I had drunk the night before. I wondered how Debbie felt and saw that it was already ten o'clock, which meant she had been at work for an hour and a half.

An alternating hot and cold shower took care of most of the headache and three cups of coffee with bacon and eggs at the coffee shop cleared the rest of it away. I silently thanked whoever it was that had told me years before that the best prevention for a hangover was to mix only water with whatever you drank and to always eat a greasy hamburger or eggs and bacon the next morning after a big night of drinking. The cure had been working well for me for the past two years.

It was almost eleven o'clock and I wondered if Debbie got off at noon for lunch. If she did and I hurried, I might catch her before she left. I paid my check and started walking towards town. Huge popcorn clouds dotted an otherwise clear blue sky and made me wonder if we might have a thunderstorm later in the day. The warm sun felt good on my back and arms as I walked the mile into town. I spotted her quickly when I got to the store where she worked. She was wearing the same Raggedy Ann suit and was still just as pretty as I remembered. She saw me and came over with a big smile.

"Hi," I said, "working hard?"

"We've been real busy," she answered, while straightening a stack of jeans that was about to topple off one of the tables and onto the sidewalk. "We have some good bargains today, some things are seventy per-cent off."

I wasn't interested in bargains, or much of anything else, except being with her at the moment. Since she was too busy for lunch we quickly confirmed that she was going to pick me up that night at seven-thirty at the motel.

With nothing else to do, I spent an hour wandering around downtown Walla Walla, had a hamburger at a local cafe, (nothing like the Palm Club hamburgers) and headed back to the motel. I lay down on the bed and instantly fell asleep. When I awoke it was already six-thirty.

I took another shower and shaved again and was just slipping on my new boots when Debbie knocked at the door.

She was stunning, wearing soft, powder blue slacks and a white sweater. The white sweater contrasted beautifully with the tan she had already acquired. I had always heard that people who lived in Washington never got sunshine but her tan went deep into the V-neck of her sweater. I caught myself wondering just how far it did go. Tonight she wore her blond hair swept back over one ear from which dangled a large gold hoop. A wide leather belt, the same color as her slacks, accentuated what I thought was the smallest waist I had ever seen on a girl. I couldn't quit looking at her until she asked, "Well, aren't you going to ask me in?"

"Sure," I stammered, "You want a drink or anything?"

"No, thanks, I had enough last night," she smiled at me.

"Well, I guess I won't have one either.

"Good, then let's go," she said, taking my arm and heading towards the door. The touch of her hand raised the hair on my forearm.

She already had the movie picked out and I wasn't surprised that it was a western with John Wayne and Ricky Nelson. I really couldn't remember anything about it since it was difficult to keep my mind on anything except her. A few minutes into the film she slipped her hand into mine, as if she had been doing it for years. After the movie she suggested we drop by Fuzzy's for a drink.

It was crowded again, with cowboys and cowgirls. I recognized a lot of the faces from the night before. Once again, Debbie was instantly recognized and room was made at a large table for us. In a room full of beautiful women she was easily the most attractive. It wasn't just her good looks that made her stand out in a crowd. Much of it was the way she handled herself and the way she had of putting people at ease. She handled a few suggestive comments from some of the cowboys with an ease that told me she was used to such talk. I found myself being a little more than jealous even though I knew I had no right to feel that way.

Although the same band was playing, we only danced to the slow songs. I held her as if she would collapse if I let her go. After about three dances, where she hadn't said much, I asked her if anything was wrong.

"No," she answered slowly, "just thinking how nice the last couple of days have been."

I agreed and offered the hope that maybe they could continue for a while longer. I wasn't worried about my job, as I knew how difficult it was to get workers at the plant. They would be particularly anxious to keep the ones they had and I knew just about anyone could walk in and start.

"You have to go back to work soon, don't you?" she asked almost in a whisper.

"Maybe tomorrow," I said, "but I can always come back if I have a reason."

"I hope so," she whispered, giving me a squeeze and a long look.

"How about if we go now," she suddenly said, looking at me with those ice blue eyes that seemed to me to be promising more than just a trip back to the motel.

"Okay, that sounds good to me," I told her, hoping I didn't sound too anxious. The truth was, I couldn't wait to be alone with her and I was beginning to wonder if the cannery would ever see me again.

I threw some money on the table for a tip and we said our good-byes to her friends.

Once in the car she said, "Let's go to my place. My roommate is gone home for a while, so no one else is there." I could only nod ok.

I tried to keep the conversation going while she was driving but she seemed to be deep in her own thoughts hardly saying anything. I wondered if her thoughts included me.

She lived in a small apartment, set back from a main house, in what appeared to be a rather wealthy neighborhood. I guessed that it was a guesthouse or maybe even servants' quarters at one time.

She came into my arms as soon as the door was closed. We hadn't even turned on the lights when her lips found mine. It was not a passionate, searching kiss, but soft yet firm, with just the tip of her tongue touching my teeth first, then my own tongue. She buried her face and lips in the space between my neck and shoulder and softly licked my skin. It was then, and still is one of the most sensual things that a woman has ever done to me.

I desperately wanted to kiss her again, but when I tried to tilt her head up, she only held me tighter and whispered, "No, not yet. I just want you to hold me for a while longer."

We must have stood like that for ten minutes, with her gently running her fingers up and down my back and softly swaying back and forth to some music that apparently only she could hear. I could hear her gently humming something that I could not understand or make out the words to. Apparently it was a song that she knew well for she continued it for the entire time we stood there holding each other.

Then, just as suddenly as she had started, and with out a word, she took one of my hands in hers and led me down a narrow hallway into a small bedroom. The room was dark and I could barely make out what was in it. As my eyes adjusted to the lack of light I could see a single bed, with lots of pillows and what I took to be small stuffed animals strewn on it and around the rest of the room. A small dresser, with the usual array of bottles and jars, was the only other thing in the room except for a large poster of a rodeo cowboy whom I recognized as last years bull riding champion.

She gave me another kiss, this time a little harder, more demanding and longer. Her hair was like silk, smelling of strawberries and lemons as it caressed my face. I held her tightly to my body, like a drowning man clinging to a sinking lifeboat. Then she stepped back and began to unbutton my shirt. I couldn't say anything because I didn't want to ruin the moment. When she had finished with the buttons, she slowly pulled it off my shoulders and dropped it on the floor. Her hands on my bare skin felt like ice. I was perspiring by this time, yet felt an involuntary shiver run down my spine. A full moon cast some light through a small window and, even in the darkness; I could see that her eyes were blue. She stepped back suddenly and with a single swift motion, pulled her sweater over her head and let it join my shirt on the floor.

"I want you now," she whispered, motioning towards the bed.

She wouldn't have to ask a second time. Together, we swept the stuffed animals off the bed. Tonight they would have to sleep on the floor.

Afterwards, she lay curled beside me and told me about herself. I had thought that she was from Walla Walla all along, but originally she was from Spokane. She had moved to Walla Walla about eight months before, because she wanted to be somewhere else, as she put it. She was twenty years old and still had most of her family living in Spokane. When she graduated from high school, she had decided not to go to college, since no one in her family ever had before.

"Do you think I was wrong?" She wanted to know.

"About what?" I asked.

"Moving away from my family and friends," she said. "Do you think people are wrong to listen to their family, or should they always try and do something that isn't acceptable? All my mother wants is for me to get married and move back to Spokane, so I can be near her and my brothers and sisters. It seems like there should be more to life than just being with family all of your life. A family always puts too many rules on you. They always see you differently than you see yourself." She was talking to me, but I got the impression she was trying to convince herself of something, although I wasn't sure just what it was. Besides, she really wasn't looking for answers from me; she just wanted someone to listen to her thoughts. I was glad it was me she had chosen.

She wanted to know about me and why I had come all the way to Washington for a summer job. I told her as much as I could. I was tired of living in the same town all of my life and wanted to see a different part of the country. I told her I wanted a little adventure and thought that hitchhiking to Washington might provide some. I told her about college, which she was interested in, asking a lot of questions about what I was going to do when I graduated and what I wanted to be doing in ten years. I had to admit that I hadn't given it much thought. She got really exited when I told her about riding bulls in summers so I could go back to college. She wanted to know if I had ever met some of the more famous cowboys, which she named. She sounded a little disappointed when I told her that most of the rodeos I rode in were much like the one in Walla Walla. I didn't tell her that the main reason I had come to Strasborg was to try and forget a lot of my past.

"You sound a lot like me." she whispered sleepily.

I had to admit that she was probably right.

She was quiet for a long time and, as her breathing became steady, I though she had fallen asleep. She moved closer and whispered: "I think we better get some sleep now, don't you?"

Maybe she could, but I knew I wasn't going to. As it turned out neither of us did for a while anyway.

I awoke the next morning to the smell of coffee brewing. For a moment I had forgotten where I was. The sight of a one-eyed teddy bear staring at me from an ice cream chair I had overlooked last night at the foot of the bed jolted me awake. The sight of the very feminine bedroom reminded me where I was and of the night before.

She came into the room carrying two large cups of coffee. She was wearing a terrycloth bathrobe, way too big for her. But it could not conceal her delicate figure. I wondered whom the robe belonged to. I wasn't sure I wanted to know the answer and wondered why I felt that way.

She sat on the edge of the bed as I reached for her, but she greeted me instead with the coffee.

"You better wake up first, don't you think?" she asked, with that big smile.

"Guess you're right," I laughed, taking the coffee, but not really wanting it at the moment.

"Whose your friend?" I pointed to the bear with my coffee cup.

"Teddy," she replied. "Not very original, I know, but he looks like a Teddy, don't you think? I've had him since I was a little girl." She picked up the worn bear and gave him a hug.

Lucky bear, I thought.

"What happened to his eye?" I asked.

"He lost it a long time ago," she said, gently rubbing the vacant spot.

"Why don't you replace it?" I was curious.

"Oh no," she cried, "This way he only sees half of what I do." She looked at me with a mischievous smile as she casually flipped the sheet off of me.

"I enjoyed last night," she said, reaching out and touching my arm, the robe sliding off her shoulders.

I spilled some of my coffee trying to set it down; it would have to wait along with my return to Strasborg.

Since it was Sunday, and I'd been absent from the plant for two days, I had to think about getting back to work. I didn't like the thought. Still, I knew I couldn't stay with Debbie forever, even though it seemed like a good idea. I had to remember work was the real reason for my stay in Washington. She didn't make it easy to do that.

Around four o'clock I finally forced myself to tell her I had to leave. She held me tighter. At six o'clock I finally got out of bed, dressed and she drove me to the edge of town, where I would try to catch a ride back to Strasborg.

She gave me a long good-bye kiss, full of promise. I told her I would call her the next week, to see if we could get together again. I didn't know how I would manage to get off work but I was prepared to think of something. I watched as she did a U-turn on the highway and headed back to town. After she was out of sight, I picked up my bag and started walking. The first car that came by stopped for me. The driver was a middle-aged man and his wife, heading for Strasborg. My luck was still running good.

I returned to an almost empty bunkhouse. Nearly everyone had gone to work or to town. The few remaining were either asleep or playing cards. I had a vague, uneasy feeling that something wasn't right. A sense of despondency overwhelmed me as heavy as the hot, humid air that enveloped Strasborg. Huge thunderclouds were rolling in the dark sky promising rain or worse as I stepped out onto the porch of the bunkhouse. The air smelled of sulfur and burnt copper.

CHAPTER VI

Monday morning began as usual, with Joe kicking me out of my bunk at five-fifteen. Lately, he seemed to be taking even more pleasure in this part of his job than any other. We were constantly being awakened by him coming in after the bars and the VFW Hall had closed. He stumbled toward his cot muttering obscenities at his enemies, real or imagined. I threw the covers back and headed for the showers. Fifteen minutes later, I was having my coffee and pancakes. Bert's cooking, like his disposition had not improved over the summer. Some of the night shift workers were coming in for breakfast, before hitting the showers.

Four Mexicans came in at the same time, even though the heavy dew the night before would delay the start of harvest until about nine or ten o'clock. The peas couldn't be picked up by the combines with heavy moisture content as it was supposed to make them mildew faster. Apparently, the Mexicans had been to a party the night before and were discussing it in conversation punctuated with laughter and a lot of arm slapping.

More of the night shift was coming into the dining hall, when the screen door was kicked open and Johnny, the smart ass who gave me my last ride to the plant, burst in. He had six of his friends with him.

Although I had seen him from a distance since my arrival, I wasn't sure if he worked at the plant or just hung around.

He and his buddies walked towards the group of Mexicans, who began to look a little worried, seeing as how they were outnumbered and outsized. The frenzied chatter they had been engaged in stopped and they all stared at their coffee cups as if no one else was around.

"Hey, Taco," Johnny yelled, pointing to the smallest of the group. "Get your wetback ass outside," he demanded in a voice that was still slurred from too much alcohol the night before. His face was flushed and he looked a little unsteady on his feet.

The Mexican kid looked at his friends and turned his palms up, indicating he didn't understand. I knew he could, however, as this was just a ploy the Mexicans often use: feigning ignorance of the language. He probably spoke better English than Johnny and his buddies if the truth were known.

"You hard of hearing, Taco?" Johnny continued. "I said, get your ass outside or I'll drag it out for you."

The kid still pretended ignorance, but there was no mistaking the fear in his eyes. He looked around the mess hall for help that wasn't there. Men busied themselves with their breakfast or turned away from the scene, which had all the makings of something ugly about to happen.

Johnny gave the kid a hard shove that sent him flying off the bench and out onto the concrete floor. He landed hard on the damp floor, sliding to the end of the table where he remained motionless. The other three Mexicans didn't move. It was probably a wise decision, since they were outnumbered almost two to one and Johnny and his gang outweighed them almost fifty pounds a man.

Bert came over, wiping his hands on a dirty dishtowel, and said in a nervous voice, "Come on, Johnny, I don't want any trouble in my kitchen. Take your problem outside if you have one."

"That's what I'm trying to do," Johnny yelled, hovering over the fallen Mexican. "Except this stinking wetback is too chicken to fight like a man. He needs to be taught a lesson about staying away from our women."

So, I thought, *that's the problem*. The Mexican had obviously been enjoying the company of some of the local ladies and Johnny was there to protect their virtue. I wondered if there was any virtue left to protect in Strasborg.

The kid made a move to get up, but at that moment he caught the full force of Johnny's boot in his rib cage and doubled over gasping for air. Smart-ass was on top of him in a flash, seeing he had the upper hand, to say nothing of his six buddies there to back him up. The sound of fist meeting flesh was ugly, as Johnny landed six or seven vicious blows to the kid's face.

Finally, Bert grabbed Johnny from behind, pinning his arms to his side as he kicked wildly at the now unconscious Mexican lying below him. Still, the other Mexicans had not moved. Nor had anyone else in the mess hall offered any assistance to the kid.

"Get him out of here," Bert ordered Johnny's friends. They seemed satisfied now that the reputation of the town's women had been saved and happy to see a little bloodshed. They took their friend by the arm and said, "C'mon, Johnny, we'll take care of the rest of them later."

Leaving the mess hall, Johnny spotted me watching him and yelled as he was leaving, "You better watch your ass, Okie, or you'll get some of the same." His face was flushed, probably more from the enjoyment of beating senseless a hapless kid, than the alcohol he had consumed. Even from a distance I could see his bloodshot eyes and the spittle at the corner of his mouth.

Realizing that seven to one odds were not in my favor, I said nothing. Besides, I was confident that just as the Mexican was left to defend himself I too would be left alone.

The three Mexicans were helping their young companion up on a bench and I went over to see if I could help. He was a mess, with blood flowing from a cut over his right eye and a huge bruise already appearing on his swollen cheek.

Wondering if it was broken, I told his friends that they better get him to the doctor in town, as I didn't see much point in stopping at the first aid station in the plant. Although men were constantly being burned or cut on the equipment there was no nurse on duty at the plant that I ever saw.

They didn't say anything. They only glared at me as if I was one of Johnny's friends. I guess I really couldn't blame them, since no one in the place had offered any assistance. I wondered, though, why none of them had tried to help their friend. Perhaps they had seen the same thing happen before and knew what the outcome would be. They probably knew the kid was going to pay the price for his indiscretion with a local girl and chalked it up to a risk taken that had gone bad.

As it turned out, the kid had a broken nose, but was back at work a day later. I couldn't imagine how he could breathe at all, working the fields with all the dust, but then I wondered how anyone could do it without a broken nose.

I went to work, feeling vaguely guilty for not intervening, but realizing full well that Johnny and his six buddies would have been only too glad to give me the same treatment they gave the Mexican. Still, I was a little ashamed of myself and no amount of rationalizing would make the feeling that maybe I should have done something more go away. I realized that I was suffering from guilt and also maybe questioning whether or not I was a coward for not standing up for what I knew was right.

The week was a miserable one with Strasborg suffering through a record heat wave with temperatures in the high nineties. The plant officials were in a hurry to get the peas in because too much heat, just like too much moisture could spoil them. They again were offering overtime to anyone who would work it but still there were no takers. The constant pushing from the foremen, coupled with the high temperature, led to short tempers. A couple of fights broke out on the floor between a crate loader and a lead man on the assembly line who thought we weren't keeping up with the pace. More men simply walked off their shift at the end of the day and didn't return the next morning.

Friday brought more humid, sweltering heat. Even having all the doors in the plant open didn't help. The steam and heat from the cooking units only added to our misery. When the six o'clock whistle blew, I was exhausted. So was everybody else. My right arm and entire shoulder was numb from the constant raking of the cans into the crate. Each day it took a little longer for the feeling to return and I wondered if I was doing permanent damage.

A cold shower helped a little, but I was not up to facing Bert's meatloaf, so I headed for the Palm Club for a cold beer and hamburger.

The club was packed with hungry, thirsty workers like myself. I ordered my usual and had the first beer finished, when May slopped my burger and fries in front of me. The beer had little rivulets of ice running down it and I drank it straight from the bottle and ordered another.

As I finished the last of my french fries I noticed several of the men going in and out of the back room and knew that the Friday night poker game was in session. I ordered a third beer and headed for the game to watch the players. The thought of sitting in on a game never entered my mind. I knew the stakes to be too high for me and I couldn't take the thought of losing two weeks' pay.

Six men sat at a round table with a naked light bulb suspended over the middle. The air was heavy with cigarette and cigar smoke. Another half dozen men stood around the players watching the action. No one spoke except for the players. I recognized Bunkhouse Joe, a regular, with his everpresent pint of Jim Beam by his side. There was Roy, a senior at Duke University, who told me he worked his way through school by gambling. He was drinking a Seven Up out of the bottle. One of the plant foremen, whose name I though was Green, was playing, along with three others that I didn't know. A rough estimate showed about two hundred dollars in the pot. I knew that on a good night, Roy had taken home over six hundred dollars. There was no doubt he was the best player. Joe never seemed to win, but he was always in the game. Roy won the hand with three sixes to two pair, held by one of the men I didn't know.

Although gambling was clearly illegal, everyone knew what went on and I had even been in the bar when the constable had come in while a game was in progress. He never visited the back room and it was understood that as long as the game remained friendly, with no sore losers, it could continue. I wondered how Joe could abide by the unwritten rules, when he was usually sullen and almost always drunk. Apparently, losing his wages meant little to him. Only Joe showed any emotion when losing, but even he was smart enough to know that creating a scene would not be tolerated.

I watched the game for a while, fascinated by the different playing styles of the men. Joe was a bluffer who seldom won a pot. He obviously didn't realize that all the players in the game understood his weakness and lack of ability. Roy was calm and cool, always seeming to know when to get out or instinctively knowing when he had the best cards. I never saw him drink anything but Seven Up during any game.

All of a sudden the bar area erupted with a commotion that carried all the way into the back room. I went back out front to see what was happening. A couple of workers from the plant had center stage and were telling about a house fire, which was apparently out of control and threatening a row of homes a few blocks away.

Most of the patrons had cleared out to go take a look at the excitement. Others, like myself, stood outside and watched the fire from a distance. It was easy to see that it was a major blaze, as the whole sky was lit up and I could see embers and ashes floating skyward as parts of buildings collapsed. Already, I could feel the heat generated from the intensity of the fire. I knew the Strasborg fire department, which consisted of one slightly antiquated fire truck with local volunteers was not going to be able to contain the blaze. It would be like pissing in hell. Someone reported the fire department from Walla Walla had been dispatched to assist, but I figured by the time they arrived it would be too late to save anything.

I watched the fire for another fifteen minutes and was getting ready to walk back to the bunkhouse, when Hassim, the Syrian, came up beside me. I had seen little of him as he worked in a different section of the plant. Like me, he seemed to be a loner, and seldom left the bunkhouse after work.

"Looks bad," he said.

"Yeah," I agreed, "Any idea of how it started?"

"Someone said it was deliberate," he said, shrugging his shoulders. "Seems someone in one of the houses saw a couple of people pouring something out of a can in back of the house right before it started. They think there may still be people in the house."

"Why would anyone do that?" I wondered out loud.

"They say the police are looking for the Mexican kid who was beaten up in the mess hall the other day," Hassim said, not looking at me.

I had a bad feeling, as I wondered whose house was burning.

"Come on," I said to Hassim, "let's go take a look."

The fire department and police were having a hard time keeping people away from the fire. I could feel the intense heat even a block away and I could see that three homes were already engulfed in flames with nothing but the shells still standing. Two other homes were on fire and the firemen were concentrating their efforts on saving them. It looked like a hopeless cause, as the fire was making rapid progress in all of them. The Walla Walla fire department had not yet arrived and the local unit was making a feeble effort to wet the surrounding houses down in hopes of preventing the fire from spreading further. For all their efforts they may as well have been using garden hoses.

The crowd displayed excitement and anger, as rumor of how the fire started to spread almost as rapidly as the blaze itself. *What is it about disasters that can also bring out the worst in people? Like those who stop to gawk at horrible car accidents*, I thought. Morbid curiosity seems to be an inherit trait in most of us, despite what we like to believe. Some were obviously enjoying the proceedings and feeling self important as they told anyone who would listen how the fire started and who was responsible. I wondered how so many could know so much about a situation that had only begun a half hour before.

I noticed Johnny, talking and gesturing wildly to a state trooper, who evidently had been called in to assist with crowd control. I moved closer to see if I could hear what he was saying.

"Fucking wetback can't run far enough to get away from me," he was saying. He was obviously drunk and the rage in his eyes and voice was scary. I could see spittle fly from his mouth when he spoke to the trooper. The patrolman was trying to calm him, but his group of buddies was there, lending encouragement and support. I sensed that more than anyone they were enjoying the chaos and the chance to be on stage.

"You don't find him, I will," he screamed, "and when I do, he's a dead Mex. Nobody burns my house and gets away with it." With that threat he and his friends stormed away.

I wondered if it was possible that the kid had started the fire to retaliate for the beating he took. In any case, I knew if the cops didn't locate him first, there would be more trouble. I wasn't too sure even the cops could protect him, seeing the crowd growing uglier each minute and encouraging Johnny.

"Let's get back to the bunkhouse," I suggested to Hassim. "We can't do anything here except be in the way." I could hear the sirens and see the flashing lights of two Walla Walla fire trucks as they made their way up the narrow street.

The bunkhouse stood nearly deserted when we got there. One of the migrant workers that I seldom saw sat on the edge of his bunk smoking a cigarette. I realized that I didn't know any of the names of the migrants, although I had been bunking with them for several weeks. *Funny*, I thought, *that I could actually live with someone for that long and not know anything about him.*

Hassim went over to him and said, "Big fire in town. I think everyone was there but you."

The Mexican, who looked to be about eighteen, just shrugged and said something I couldn't understand.

Hassim came back over and said, "I don't think he is friends with the others, but he better have a good alibi. I hope someone was here with him when the fire started. That bunch at the fire doesn't really care who they get as long as someone pays."

He went outside to stand on the porch and watch the fire which now lit up the entire western sky. Huge flames shot far into the night air sending up black smoke and cinders from the ashes of the homes which it had consumed.

A car with one headlight was coming up the road at far too fast a speed as I looked out the window of the bunkhouse. It came sliding to a stop in front of the bunkhouse and Johnny and his friends piled out and raced inside.

The migrant kid sat still on his bunk as Hassim went back inside to see what was going to happen. Johnny and his friends headed straight for him. The kid made a move to get up, but Johnny grabbed him by the back of his hair and yanked savagely while two of his buddies held the kid's arms tight behind his back.

"Okay, Mex," Johnny seethed, with a voice heavy from the alcohol and whatever else he may have had, "where're your wetback friends?"

The kid didn't say a thing, only looking coolly back at Johnny. A hard blow to the stomach doubled him over and again Johnny yanked his head back.

"I ain't asking you again, Mex," Johnny yelled in his face.

"He doesn't know anything," I interrupted. I was surprised to find my voice calm, although I was nervous inside.

Still holding the kid by the hair, Johnny turned to look at me with eyes that were just narrow slits. He wavered a little on his feet and glared at me as if trying to focus in on my voice.

"Watch him," he indicated the kid to his buddies with a hard shove to the Mexican's chest.

He walked slowly towards me, unsteady on his feet from all of the alcohol he had consumed that day. "Maybe you know something about all of this, huh, Okie?" He breathed his rotten breath on me, not more than six inches from my face. I could smell the sour odor of beer, and cigarettes from the sweat than ran down his face and collected on his chin.

"Maybe this is the guy we want," he said, turning to his friends. "You seem to like wetbacks," he growled, turning back to stare at me. "Maybe we should talk to the Okie and his black buddy here," he continued, motioning his friends to come over for help. Like all cowards and bullies, Johnny was not going to make a move unless he had plenty of support.

"How about it, Okie?" He jabbed me in the chest with a short, stubby finger, which I could see was stained yellow from too much nicotine.

I took a step backward hoping to get in at least one good punch before his friends arrived and I got the same treatment as the Mexican kid in the mess hall. Johnny advanced with his fist raised.

I didn't see the knife until the tip of it was under Johnny's chin, with just enough pressure to make him rise on his toes. He stopped suddenly like a dog being yanked on a leash. His eyes rolled to the side trying to discover the source of his discomfort.

"We already told you," Hassim was saying, "nobody here knows anything about the fire or who started it." The six-inch blade moved a little higher and Johnny rose a little higher on his toes. He made no effort to move and kept his arms limp at his side. The knife, I could see was the switchblade variety with a razor edge that glittered in the semi-darkness of the bunkhouse.

By this time, three or four other day workers had come into the bunkhouse, along with Joe. I was never happier to see him than at that moment.

"What's going on here?" Joe mumbled, drunk as usual. "Ain't going to be no trouble here," he yelled. "You bastards got differences, you settle them somewhere else besides my bunkhouse."

Johnny started to protest, but with six inches of cold steel under his chin it was difficult. Joe sensed he had the upper hand and the backing of most everyone there who was tired of Johnny and his buddies.

"You get outa here now, Johnny," he yelled, pointing a grubby gnarled finger towards the door.

The group of them moved towards the door with the rest of us following. Like most bullies they had lost their courage when the odds were even. Johnny turned back to face us, once he was outside, and pointing his finger at me he shouted, "You and your Mex friends have had it Okie. You're all dead meat, you understand me? I'll be back. This ain't over yet."

We watched until the car roared out of sight. We knew it wasn't over by a long shot. It never is with people like Johnny.

"He is a dangerous person," Hassim offered quietly. "I think you better watch out for a while."

"You didn't exactly make friends with him," I said. "You made him look bad in front of his buddies. I don't think he will forget that." I knew that for people like Johnny, humiliation was something that he could never accept. Being exposed for the real coward that he was would eat away at him until he got revenge.

Hassim could only nod in agreement as he closed the knife blade and slid it in his pocket.

We went inside to see what we could do for the Mexican kid, who was still looking bewildered by the whole incident. He seemed to be ok as he was sitting on his bunk smoking another cigarette.

"I think maybe it's a good idea if one of us stays awake for the rest of the night," I said to Hassim. "Just in case they decide to come back later."

"I believe you are right," He agreed, stretching out on his cot and lighting up a cigarette.

We talked for a couple of hours until midnight and agreed that I would take the first watch, until two, and then wake him.

I tried to read, but couldn't see the pages, then I walked around, but knew I was disturbing those trying to sleep. Finally, I stretched out on my bunk about a quarter to two.

I was so tired from the week of work and the events of the past few hours that I immediately fell asleep. I dreamed of Nancy, and Leigh, and Debbie. But first, last and always of Nancy. How to forget. That had been my problem for two years, but I still didn't have the answer. I still wouldn't have it twenty years later. I tried but with no success. I drank a lot, went out with other girls, and rebelled against everything I knew was right and good. It was my way, the only way I knew. How was I supposed to forget something and someone I never wanted to? If you forget, then a part of you dies. I didn't want it to die. I wanted her memory. I wanted to remember her smell, her laugh, and her touch. I wanted her. I knew it wouldn't happen. It all seemed so long ago and far away. That was where I was now. Long ago and far away from her. But she was there, always there, like a hard rain that drives at you from every direction, not letting you turn away from it, pounding at you from all directions as if to say, "You can't ignore me. I won't go away. You have to deal with me and what I'm doing to you."

Drinking became my answer. Every day, whatever I could, with anyone who wanted to. Until one day someone asked me who she was and why I was trying so hard to forget. I didn't know it showed so much. People who wallow in their own misery seldom do.

So I came to Washington, two thousand miles away, to try and forget. It didn't work. I missed her every day, every hour and minute. But life goes on. I was here. She was there, somewhere, never far away from me and my thoughts.

And so I dreamed of valleys full of giants, of long summer days and hot nights. Of high school basketball games and her in a red sweater and a perfect smile waiting for me. Of hours spent parked on lonely country roads, holding her close and planning for the future. Except now the future was just what happened today and maybe tomorrow. I had begun to believe that my future didn't exist except perhaps in a dream.

I dreamed of those for whom there would never be a future. Of my best friend, dead at fifteen. And of Cindy. Dear, sweet, lovable Cindy, who wanted nothing more than to enjoy her life each and every day. Gone in the few fleeting seconds that it takes a careless driver to lose control of his car and send her dreams, hopes and goals into an empty eternity. But always I dreamed of her, only to awaken to discover that while life does indeed go on, so do the dreams.

I awoke to footsteps on the porch at the far end of the bunkhouse. I rose up, trying to adjust my eyes to the darkness just in time to see Johnny's outline in the doorway. He was holding a bottle with a burning rag stuffed into it. Without a word, he hurled it into the end of the bunkhouse towards the cot where the Mexican kid was sleeping.

The whole east end of the building was immediately awash in flames as the gasoline ignited bunks, clothing and the dry wooden floor of the old bunkhouse. Years of accumulated grease and grime coupled with the dry air made it nothing more than a tinderbox ready to explode.

Hassim was awake almost as soon as I was. We started screaming for everyone to get up, as unbelievably some of the workers were still asleep. Suddenly, a figure came running through the flames at the far end of the bunkhouse with his hair on fire and the lower half of what had been his pajamas already burned off. The figure made a full turn as if looking for something he had lost, then, in what appeared to me slow motion, started a slow staggering walk towards the door, arms spread wide and held upward trying to escape the intense heat and fire which now totally engulfed him. The stench of burning hair and flesh was already wafting through the bunkhouse.

By now everyone was awake and running towards the exit. People were falling over cots and each other as some grabbed for shoes or jackets. Most abandoned everything however, and raced outside, several falling over the porch railing onto the hard ground below. Crazily, I remember thinking to myself if this was what hell looked like as flames raced hungrily up the walls and began to shoot out the top of the building.

Hassim had stripped a blanket off his cot and rushing towards the burning figure, tackled him near the doorway. I was right behind him when I realized Joe was still in his corner bunk. Passed out in his drunken stupor, he was not even aware that the place was literally burning down around him. I ran over and punched him hard in the chest while trying to drag him out of his cot. He only grunted and flung out a meaty arm at me. I knew I couldn't wake him and the fire was spreading quickly in the rotten floor and walls of the bunkhouse. The whole north end was now a wall of flames, as the fire seemed to leap frog from one cot to the next.

I yelled for Hassim to come and help me. Together, we managed to lift Joe out of his cot, which I thought to myself was like trying to lift a two hundred-pound sack of Jello. He was coming around now however, cursing at us for being too noisy. Flailing his arms wildly he caught me full force on the side of the head with one of his huge hands and I felt my ears pop. I grabbed his arm and slapped him as hard as I could. I wasn't doing it as much in anger as I was in trying to get him awake.

"Come on Joe," I screamed, "the bunkhouse is on fire. We have to get out of here now."

"Where's my shoes?" he demanded to know.

"Forget them, man," Hassim yelled, putting one arm around his shoulders and lifting. I got under the other shoulder and together, we half carried, half dragged the old drunk outside where all three of us went tumbling off the steps headfirst onto the ground.

About twenty workers were standing around in various stages of undress, most of them only in jeans and tee shirts and no shoes. Amazingly, there were already a number of townspeople gathered and, in the distance; I could hear the fire engine. Two fires in one night. The people of Strasborg would have something to talk about for a long time.

The bunkhouse was almost totally engulfed now. Flames had already shot through the roof of the old building as it began to collapse. The tarpaper used to line the walls only provided fuel for the fire. The smoke and ashes from the bunkhouse now mingled with those from the earlier fire. Few people were talking, as most of the men watched their meager possessions burn. I noticed a blanket covering a body a few feet away from us and looked at Hassim.

"The Mexican kid," he answered my silent question. "He didn't make it." Apparently someone had dragged him out after Hassim and I had returned to get Joe out of his bunk.

The old fire truck arrived, but there was little to do, except watch, as the building was beyond any thought of saving. The firemen decided it would be best to let it burn completely. They directed water to the edges of the building and the surrounding railroad tracks to keep the sparks from spreading.

"Funny," I said to Hassim, "I always thought Strasborg was hell, now it sure looks like it."

He only stared at me, as if he thought maybe I was crazy. Maybe, at that time, I was.

An ambulance had arrived and began loading the Mexican kid into a body bag. While they were moving him, the blanket slipped off and I saw why he never had a chance. The bottle of gasoline must have landed squarely on top of his bunk as he lay sleeping in it. Maybe he inhaled the first few flames into his lungs. He was probably dead by the time Hassim had reached him. I hoped so. The ambulance workers finished their job and then checked to see if anyone else needed attention. Except for a few scrapes and bruises from falling off the porch no one else had been injured in the fire. The porch began to sag as the fire ate away its support posts and then came crashing down, sending a huge shower of sparks into the still night air.

The cops also had arrived and began to take statements from everyone, after getting the group quieted down. Apparently, I was the only eyewitness to exactly what had happened. No one else had seen anything, as they had all been asleep. I told them what I saw.

"You sure?" The young cop asked, when I told him it was Johnny who had thrown the bottle of gasoline. "It was pretty dark. How can you be sure who you saw?" the cop wanted to know.

"I'm sure," I told him. "Put it down. It was Johnny."

It wasn't a scene I was likely to forget, as I remembered the look on his drunken face when he hurled the flaming liquid directly at the kid's bunk. It wasn't a look of hatred I saw on his face. What I saw was ignorance and fear. Ignorance of other people and fear of losing control of the only existence he had ever known. Strangely enough, I didn't feel hatred at the moment, only a kind of sadness that people like Johnny and his friends even existed in a place that already had too much sadness in it. People like Johnny couldn't accept any changes in their life and they were prepared to defend it the only way they knew how. Through lies, bigotry, violence and hatred, they would carry on. I wondered to myself how much we were all a little like him and his friends.

I also wondered if there was any way the Mexican kid would even have his relatives notified. He was obviously an illegal, as were most of the migrants. Poor bastard would probably be buried by the county and his family would never even know about it. Since he was illegal, there most likely would be no money available to ship the body back to Mexico. Besides, no one seemed to know where he came from, so there wasn't much else to do.

Someone mentioned that the company would probably be in trouble, now that a murder had occurred and there would have to be an investigation. I wasn't so sure than anything would happen. The plant hired illegals, but that fact was conveniently overlooked by the authorities because it operated under an extremely tight schedule, and without enough local labor to run the operation during the harvest. The company found it profitable to hire illegals at half the normal pay, and house them in company bungalows while charging them rent, which was withheld from their pay. While Strasborg did not have company housing the town of Hayden, which also had a factory, had numerous families living in company owned bungalows. This way, most of them ended up working for little more than room and board. Some of the young men chose to live in tents or cars near the edge of town, by a small stream that provided them with water for bathing. Some of them, like the kid who just died, lived in the bunkhouse. *Too bad he hadn't stayed with the others*, I thought. *He might still be alive.*

After the pea harvest, most of them would pick fruit in the Yakima Valley of Washington and then on down the coast of California, eventually ending up in Mexico to wait until the next harvest season. Such a system was tolerated, since officials knew the Mexicans would work cheap at the dirtiest jobs, with no real threat to anyone else's job. I was reminded again of how much they were like the broomcorn johnnies in my own hometown. Traveling almost all the year working at menial, back breaking labor the jobs must have seemed like a wonderful opportunity to escape the grinding poverty they knew in their own country. I had traveled almost two thousand miles in hopes of finding something different and positive. Now, it seemed that most things in life were the same regardless of where I was.

Hassim and I walked to the mess hall with the other men to spend the rest of the night and wait for morning. The night air was chilly after we left the intense heat from the fire and I wished that I had a jacket. Like everyone else, I had lost all my clothing except what I was wearing. The cafeteria was being used as a sort of clearinghouse by the sheriff and local cops to collect more statements from all of those who were in the bunkhouse when the fire started.

The sheriff took the place of the young cop and took a detailed statement from me and Hassim, asking me if I was sure it was Johnny that I saw toss the firebomb. I was certain of that fact. I could tell he was hoping I would change my mind.

"You know," he drawled, looking at both of us, "that you will have to testify if this goes to trial. Could be that you would have to come all the way back to Strasborg to do that," he concluded with raised eyebrows. "Be a real shame to have to leave college to do that, if you're not sure who you saw, now wouldn't it boys?"

The sheriff continued. "Might mean that you can't even leave here, if you stand by this story." He tapped his pencil against his teeth.

Hassim and I looked at each other. I think we both knew that by sundown we planned to be a long way from Strasborg and all the good old boys in it.

"You boys think about it," the sheriff said with a long sigh, indicating his displeasure with us for identifying one of the locals as the culprit. " I'll talk to you both tomorrow, if you're still around," he added, hitching up his gun belt around an ample belly.

I knew then for a certainty that charges were never going to be filed against Johnny and his buddies. Besides, if they were, it would just be a formality. My word against theirs. I was sure he could produce a dozen witnesses to testify that he was nowhere near the bunkhouse the night of the fire.

Hassim knew what I was thinking, for he said, "I don't believe this place is healthy for the two of us. I'm leaving as soon as I can see daylight."

I nodded in agreement.

We spent the rest of the night drinking coffee and discussing our plans. Hassim intended to go back to college, same as me. He was certain that we would never be called to testify. "Do you think," he asked, "that they would take my word? Look at me. I'm not the right color. Not even close."

I felt a certain amount of guilt, knowing that Johnny might walk away free with murder on his hands but, as Hassim pointed out, I knew Johnny would have plenty of people to testify on his behalf. We couldn't do anymore than what we had just done. The system was wrong, but I knew for sure that two outsiders were not going to change it. We were in a community that had only one set of rules and they operated for the people in the town and factory. What was good for the factory was good for the people and vice versa. Everything revolved around the plant and a successful harvest. Nothing would be allowed to happen that would jeopardize the completion of the season. The show must go on, never mind that workers had been displaced and a murder had taken place. I realized that people like Hassim and myself were only tolerated as necessary cogs in the machinery, to keep the plant running smoothly. We didn't live in the town, therefore, we didn't exist. Neither did our statements to the police. I knew, in my heart they would never be produced for any district attorney. I was beginning to understand how Tom Joad must have felt. I thought: *Just another Okie in the wrong place at the wrong time.*

Even though the bunkhouse was burned down, with all of the worker's possessions in it, the plant would continue to operate. Quick arrangements were made with the local high school to use the gymnasium as quarters. The company brought in cots and blankets, so it was really going to be no different than the bunkhouse as far as facilities were concerned. I had no desire to stay for the end of the pea season, which would be over in a couple of weeks anyway.

The personnel office opened the next morning at seven o'clock, an hour after the plant did. *Business as usual,* I thought. Hassim and I walked over to give them our resignations and collect our checks and were surprised to see a half dozen other men already there ahead of us. Apparently, we weren't the only ones who had enough of peas, hot weather, ugly women and now murder.

A few minutes after seven, the plant foreman came in and

announced that there would be a delay in getting our checks, since there were so many of us quitting at the same time. He suggested we might want to work that day and pick up our checks later. We all knew they were going to be shorthanded without us, but no one was willing to work another day. Despite the fact that a murder had been committed and peoples' possessions destroyed, the only real concern was to see that ten thousand cases of peas were processed that day.

The foreman announced that he was authorized to give twenty cents an hour bonus to anyone who would stay and finish the season. He was met with a round of stony silence. After seeing that we all were determined to leave as soon as possible, he mumbled something about "seeing what I can do" and we all went back to the mess hall for more of Bert's bad coffee. About an hour later, one of the clerks came in and told us our final checks were ready.

Hassim and I said our good-byes and decided, since we would both be hitchhiking out of town, it might be better to split up, with one of us going ahead. Pat had already left town several days earlier as he had tired of the back-breaking work quickly. I decided to wait an hour and then follow Hassim We shook hands and made the usual promises about looking each other up if we ever got close to our respective colleges. We both knew that would probably never happen. In many ways, the two of us were as different as we were from the townspeople of Strasborg. Still, when he held the knife under Johnny's chin, I had discovered what it was like to be a real outsider. To be considered a threat to everyone who had a different opinion of people and life. I knew then I was only tolerated because of my willingness to work the long hours without question and for little pay. Ashamed of myself for thinking it, I wondered if Hassim had done it because he truly liked me. Or was he just taking out his frustrations on Johnny and all those like him that he had no doubt met over and over in his lifetime. Whatever the reason, I felt kinship with Hassim that I had never felt towards anyone before. Although I had grown up poor, for the first time in my life I had been truly different, and knew the feeling of being alone and helpless. I didn't like to think about what the outcome of that night would have been like if he hadn't been there, ready to stand beside me. I wondered what I would have done if the situation had been reversed. I want to believe that I would have done the same for him. Hassim was gone and so would I be in another hour.

I decided to kill time by dropping into the Palm Club. Even though it was only a little past nine in the morning, there were already half dozen regulars having coffee and a couple already nursing their first beer of the day.

The topic of conversation of course, was the big fire the preceding night. As always, rumors were rampant and one of the men was saying he understood it was Mexicans who started the bunkhouse fire as some sort of revenge.

"Always knew it was a mistake to hire them wetbacks," he allowed, with the air of self-importance some people take on when they are enjoying discussing other people's misery. Most of the others chimed in with nods or some sort of endorsement.

One of the men picked up his coffee and settled onto the stool next to me.

"Don't you work at the plant?" He wanted to know.

"Not anymore," I answered, hoping he would go away.

"Quit, huh?"

"This morning," I said. I wasn't in the mood for lengthy discussion.

"You in the bunkhouse last night?" He continued his interrogation.

"Yes," I said, sipping my coffee, "I was there."

"See how it started," he asked, swirling his coffee around in the cup, avoiding looking at me.

I had a pretty good idea what he was getting at and I didn't want any more confrontations with local heroes.

"I told the sheriff everything I saw," I answered, not looking at him.

"So I heard, but some of us ain't convinced you saw what you said you did." He was leaning closer to me and I could smell the foul odor of his coffee breath and dentures.

"I saw it," I told him. "Now it's up to the police to investigate."

"Yeah," he said, giving me a toothy grin, "it's up to the authorities to investigate it now." He gave me a little tap on the shoulder to make sure I got his point.

His smile and emphasis on authorities left little doubt about the outcome of any investigation.

I knew for certain now that nothing would happen to Johnny. There would be so many of the good town folks more than willing to supply him with an alibi that the case would never get beyond where it was now.

I slid off the bar stool, picked up my change and headed for the door. The guy who was so concerned about what I saw twirled around on his bar stool with his arms folded across his fat belly and said, "You have a good trip home now, you hear."

I never looked back as I wanted nothing more than to be home right now. But first I was going to make a stop in Walla Walla to see Debbie.

CHAPTER VII

After I reached the highway a trucker coming down from Spokane stopped for me. Half an hour later I was in Walla Walla.

I headed straight for the department store where Debbie worked. I thought maybe I could catch her for lunch. I wandered around for a couple of minutes, hoping to see her, when an overly made up sales clerk stopped and asked if she could be of any help.

"Yes, is Debbie working today?" I asked her.

"Oh, Debbie doesn't work here any longer," she replied with a big smile.

"Do you know where she is?" I asked her.

"Why yes, she moved back to Spokane. I understand she may be getting married," she said with a bigger smile and a little wink.

"Thank you," I managed to stammer as I turned to leave.

"Married," I said to myself. Well why not. Most girls eventually do I suppose. Still, I couldn't help but think about the time we had spent together and wonder about her commitment to marriage.

On the way out of the store, I passed through the children's department and spotted a huge display of teddy bears. *Well*, I thought, *if she was getting married, a wedding present was in order*. I picked up a soft brown teddy bear with a red felt tongue hanging out of its mouth and headed back towards the sales clerk who had given me the news.

I spotted her busily rearranging some women's blouses. Walking up to her, I asked if she might have an address in Spokane for Debbie.

"Why certainly," she answered, "we have to send her last paycheck there. She left in such a hurry; she didn't have time to collect it. Come with me," she ordered.

She took me to an office in back and pulled a file folder from a cabinet.

"Here it is," she said, copying it down for me and handing me the piece of paper.

"Could I get this wrapped and sent to her?" I asked, indicating the teddy bear.

"I'll be glad to take care of that for you," she said, still flashing her big smile. "Would you like a card to go with that?" She wanted to know.

I handed her the bear and accepted the card, wondering just what to say.

"Just a minute," I said, taking the bear back from her. With a pair of scissors which were lying on the countertop, I snipped one of the bear's eyes out. I handed it back to the woman who was looking at me as if I had just mutilated Smokey the Bear.

I wrote on the card, "Now you have a pair." I handed it to the sales clerk, who was still inspecting the injured bear.

"Don't you want to sign your name?" she asked me, after reading the card.

"No, I think not," I told her, handing over money for the bear and gift-wrapping. I left her still pondering the maimed bear and the card.

I stopped on my way out and bought a jacket, a couple of shirts, a canvas bag and pair of jeans to replace the ones I had lost in the fire.

It was a good two-mile walk to the main highway, which would take me back on the road home. I spent the time reliving the two nights I had spent with Debbie and hoping that she would be happy. I recalled our conversation about family and how their expectations for their children always seemed to be in conflict with our own. I hoped that she could make some kind of peace with hers. I was glad to have something to think about besides Strasborg but I knew I could never forget what had happened there. For a time I had thought that all the bad features that people possess could be found in that sad, lonely little town. I now realized that the people there were no different than anyone else, living anywhere else.

Setting my packages by the side of the road I pulled my new windbreaker tighter against the sudden chill of the mountain air. I stuck out my thumb as traffic approached.

Off in the distance, I could see a hard rain beginning to fall.

Printed in the United States
86076LV00006B/16/A